THE BILLIONAIRE GLITCH DATE

BILLIONAIRE ONLINE DATING SERVICE BOOK #6

ELLE JAMES

TWISTED PAGE INC

THE BILLIONAIRE GLITCH DATE

BILLIONAIRE ONLINE DATING SERVICE BOOK #6

New York Times & USA Today
Bestselling Author

ELLE JAMES

Dedicated to my husband who understands when I need to write like my hair is on fire and clears the path for me to do so!
Elle James

"ALL RIGHT, we're all here. What's up?" Dillon Jacobs asked his little sister Emma as he and his three brothers sat around the shiny black conference table in the high-rise executive offices of the Billionaire Online Dating Service.

Emma stood hand in hand with her new husband, Billionaire Frank Cooper Johnson. She turned to Leslie Lamb, the owner of the exclusive match-making company and nodded. "I've asked Leslie to help each of you find your perfect match using BODS."

Her brother Colton held up both hands. "Whoa there, little sis. Who says we need help finding our perfect mate?"

"That's right," Dillon backed up his brother. "I thought you brought us here to talk us into investing in Leslie's little venture."

Leslie smiled. "I don't need additional investment capital. The system is generating a sustainable income stream. I really am here to help you all find your matches."

Brand shook his head. "I'm out. Once bitten and all that. Matches, mates and marriages give me the hives."

Ace, who'd been standing by the door, crossed to stand beside Emma. "Our sister has our best interests at heart. She and Coop want to start a family."

"That's right," Emma said, a smile spilling across her face. "And I want my children to grow up with cousins their own age." She pointed to each of her brothers. "In order to do that, each of you needs to quit stalling and man-up to the challenge of finding wives."

"That's some serious talk for a woman who only a short time ago didn't want to date," Brand said, his lips twitching.

"And my meddling brothers forced me into it," she said crossing her arms over her chest. "It's my turn to meddle now, and you four men are going to give BODS a go. It worked for me and Coop and all of Coops friends. It'll work for you," she said, her chin held high with confidence.

Ace grimaced, but then shrugged. "Look, it's not going to hurt any of us to give Leslie's online dating service a try."

"If you're so set on doing this," Dillon said, a smile playing at the corners of his lips, "you can go first."

Ace's mouth stretched into a grin. "I offered, but Emma thought of a way to make it fair deciding who goes first. She brought straws from the ranch. Whoever draws the shortest straw wins."

Brand frowned. "You mean loses."

"No," Ace said. "I meant what I said. Short straw wins the opportunity to go first."

"For this round," Emma said. "Remember, I was the first of the Jacob family to try Leslie's system. And you all know how successful the results were." She leaned into Coop. "Tell them."

Coop grinned. "Guys, I would not have met and fallen in love with your beautiful sister if not for BODS. The system matched us perfectly. You should give it a shot. At the very least, you'll go on a date."

Emma's eyes narrowed, and she looked at each of her brothers, one at a time. "When was the last time any one of you went on a date?"

"I went on one last Saturday," Brand said.

Emma snorted. "Picking up a one-night stand at the Ugly Stick Saloon doesn't count. It wasn't a real date, and do you even remember her name?"

"Of course I do," Brand said. "It was...Susan, I think."

"Her name was Desiree, you dufus," Colton said. "And you haven't asked a woman out on a real date in forever."

"Not since before you married the wicked witch of the west, Bridgett," Ace said. "That's been over four years. You need to move on."

"I don't need a wife," Brand said. "They're high maintenance and cost too much in the long run."

"That's what prenups are for," Colton said.

"Didn't think I'd need one," Brand muttered.

"Yeah, and she cleaned you out, didn't she?" Dillon said. "Where are the straws, Emma? Let's get this show on the road. I have a project falling behind as we speak. Come on, long straw. I don't have time for this right now."

Emma held out her hand curled around four hay straws that appeared to all be the same length. The bottoms were hidden beneath her fingers.

Emma swung her hand toward Ace. "Oldest first."

Ace drew a straw and looked at it. The straw was approximately three inches in length. "Is this a long one or a short one?"

"Guess you'll have to wait and see," Emma said with a sly grin.

Brand drew next, his straw longer than Ace's. He whooped. "Ha! You'll have to play guinea pig this round, bro."

"We're not finished yet," Emma said.

Colton took the next one and grinned. "Mine is even longer than Brand's." He wiped his hand across his forehead. "Dodged that bullet."

"Which leaves one more straw." Emma turned to Dillon. "Your turn."

"Sucks to be the youngest brother," Dillon muttered. "Next time we should start drawing straws from youngest to oldest."

"Take the damned straw," Ace said.

Dillon yanked the straw out of Emma's hand and swore. His straw was only two inches long. The shortest of all four straws. "I really don't have time for this right now."

"Yeah, but you're the one who said you wanted to get started on your own place and have it ready for when you found a bride to bring home to it," Ace said.

"He said that?" Emma's eyes widened, a smile spreading across her face. "Then this is perfect timing."

"No," Dillon said. "Perfect timing would be after I build my house. Not before I even break ground."

"It takes time to woo a woman," Emma said.

"Precisely my point," Dillon said. "The construction project I'm supervising is on the verge of falling behind. I promised I'd have it completed by the end of the month. That's only three weeks from now. I don't have time to date." He held out his hand with the short straw. "Someone take my turn. I'll do the next round."

Each brother leaned back in his chair, hands up.

"Dude, you're it," Ace said with a grin.

"Your turn will be soon enough," Emma said. "You're all going to do this if I have to hold your hands through the data entry process."

Dillon raked a hand through his hair. "Sweet Jesus, how long is the data entry process? I have subs to call and a construction site to visit tonight."

"If you'll quit belly-aching and get started, it'll take less than an hour." She glanced out the window of the high-rise. "And you're not going to any construction site tonight because it'll be raining, if those storm clouds are any indication."

"Damn," Dillon said. "I knew I should have gone there first."

"And break your promise to your only sister?" Emma's lips twisted. "Come on. Leslie will show you to the computer room where you can enter your data. I'll help you get started, but then Coop and I have a reservation at Perry's tonight. My mouth's been watering for steak all day."

Dillan brightened. "Then you fill out my questionnaire, and I'll go eat steak with Coop."

"Sorry, man. It's date night," Coop said with a twisted grin. "You're not my type."

Dillon grumbled beneath his breath. "Fine. I'll fill out the questionnaire."

"And you'll have an open mind...?" Emma coaxed.

Dillon never could resist his little sister. "I'm not against this whole dating service. I'm just up against a bitch of a deadline."

Ace pushed to his feet and clapped a hand on his brother's shoulder. "Maybe having a woman in your life will help relieve some of that stress."

"Fuck you, Ace." Dillon shoved his brother's hand off his shoulder. "You're not the one having to stay to fill out the questionnaire."

"No, I'm not." Ace grinned. "But my time is coming. For now, I need to get back out to the ranch and batten down the hatches before that storm hits."

Brand stared out at the darkening sky. "Don't think you're going to make it. Looks like it's already raining west of the city. Which means it's probably already raining at the ranch."

Ace grinned. "Then I might as well join Emma and Coop at the steakhouse."

"You heard the man," Colton said. "They're going out on a date. No brothers allowed."

"Then you, me and Brand can hit the Firehouse Lounge for drinks. Dillon can join us when he's done painting a pretty picture of himself for the girls." Ace winked and headed for the door.

Emma and Leslie each hooked one of Dillon's arms.

Dillon frowned down at them. "You're not ganging up on me, are you?"

Emma grinned. "Nope. We just want to get you started so we can get going. Remember? I have a date."

"And I have another client arriving any minute,"

7

Leslie said glancing at her watch. "I want to get you logged on, and your picture taken for your profile, before I leave you to your questionnaire."

"I'm sure I can figure it out," Dillon said. "How hard can it be to take a photo?"

"You'd be surprised how many clients can't get their faces in the center." Leslie led him into a small, comfortable room with a padded, white leather chair, white desk and a computer. She pulled the chair out and pointed. "Sit."

"Yes, ma'am." Dillon took the seat, feeling more like a trained dog than a candidate for her dating service.

In a few short minutes, Leslie had the system up, Dillon's logon created, and a decent photo saved to his profile. She brought up the questionnaire and stepped back. "The rest is up to you. You can enter as much or as little as you like, but the more information about yourself, your likes and dislikes you enter into the system, the better chances of the software finding your perfect match."

"So, don't sell yourself short," Emma said with a stern look. "You're a great guy, and some woman is going to be lucky to find you. Please, give it your best." She kissed his cheek. "You know I love you, and I want you to be as happy as I am. And remember, you pushed me into dating when I didn't think I ever wanted to again."

Dillon squeezed his sister's hand. "You were dealt

a pretty rough blow when Marcus died in Afghanistan. But now, you have Coop."

"Exactly. And you could find someone to love as well. If you give BODS a chance." Emma hugged her brother and stepped back. "Now, I have to go. Be sure to put all your good attributes in there. Some lucky lady is going to get a wonderful guy."

Leslie crossed to the door. "I'm going to get my other client set up. Then I'm out of here. I have to drop my car off at the dealership before they close. All you have to do is fill out the questionnaire. When you leave, just pull the office door shut. It will lock automatically."

"You trust your clients to close up shop?" Dillon asked.

"I screen my clients before I invite them to enter my system," Leslie said. "Besides. I know where you live." She gave him a big smile. "You're a good guy."

Emma and Leslie left Dillon in the room, closing the door behind them.

Dillon sighed and focused on the monitor. "Name. Dillon Jacobs. Age. Old enough to know better." He chuckled, glanced at his watch, and then got busy answering the questions. He hoped the woman he was matched with would be punctual, orderly, well-kempt, a business professional who could whip up a spreadsheet with her eyes closed, early riser, liked dogs and who also liked to ride horses. After all, if things did work out—which he wasn't convinced they would—she'd be living with him on the ranch. Oh, and she should be tall so he wouldn't have to bend down too far to kiss her. He pressed enter to save his profile, straightened the keyboard and mouse and pushed back his chair to stand when a huge crash of thunder rattled the building.

Damn. He needed to get to the Firehouse Lounge before the sky opened up. Dillon hurried toward the door.

CHAPTER 2

ARIANA DAVIS WAITED at the empty reception desk of her friend Leslie Lamb's office. As Leslie had mentioned, Ava, their friend and the receptionist wasn't there, having taken off the afternoon to go with her daughter to the dentist.

The logo on the front of the desk read BODS. She frowned, wondering what BODS stood for and regretting coming. She would have turned and left, but she'd promise Leslie that she'd at the very least give her dating service a try.

One date.

Her pulse kicked up a notch, and her breathing grew slightly ragged at the thought.

"I'm not ready for this," she murmured, feeling her anxiety level rising.

Using some of the techniques she'd learned about meditation, and now taught at her studio, she inhaled deeply, closed her eyes and pictured a placid lake where the water was still, the moon reflected off the surface and all was calm.

Her heartbeat slowed, and she breathed normally again.

"Ariana, I'm so glad you came." Leslie's voice pierced the placid lake and brought Ariana back to the office and the reason she'd come.

Opening her eyes, Ariana forced a smile to her lips. "I have to admit, I almost called to say I couldn't come."

Leslie's brow wrinkled. "Oh, sweetie. Are you that worried about dating again?" She came around the desk and pulled Ariana into her arms. "We all talked about it at the Good Grief Club meeting. You won't completely move on with your life if you don't get back out there."

Ariana signed. "But it's such a crap shoot. I'll never find a man as sweet and perfect for me as Sam was." Her eyes welled with the ready tears.

"I know you feel that way. Emma felt the same about Marcus and look how happy she is with Coop. We'll find someone for you. Trust me."

"What scares me is the thought of finding someone else and losing him, too," Ariana said. "I think it's safer to live alone than to give my heart away a second time, only to have it broken all over again."

"You can't live life expecting the worse," Leslie said softly. "You don't teach that at your studio, do you?" She took Ariana's arm and walked her around the desk to the hallway leading into her suite of offices. "No, you don't," she answered for her. "You help your clients to see the beauty in life that makes it worth living. You show them how to let go of the things they can't change and change the things they can. You help them find their mental balance as well as their physical balance."

"Life is all about balance," Ariana said, nodding. "When you lose someone you love, it shifts the balance."

"And it's up to the individual to redefine their balance." Leslie grinned. "I learned that from you. In your yoga class."

Ariana smiled. "I said that, didn't I?" She drew in a deep breath. "Change can be good. But not all change can be controlled." Her brow furrowed. "Sam proved that. Since his death, I try not to let the little things bother me."

"You can think of my dating service as a little thing. Don't let it bother you. Let the system do the work of finding the right person for you."

"To date," Ariana stated. "I'm only promising to go on one date. I'm not ready for anything else."

"One date," Leslie agreed. "You'll see. BODS will match you with the right person. It's up to you if you want to see him after the first date." Leslie squeeze her arm. "I'm certain you'll be happy with the results and want to see more of him."

"One date," Ariana insisted. "That's all I'm promising."

"Okay." Leslie guided her past an open door to a conference room with a large dark table and white leather chairs all around it. She passed a closed door on the left and stopped at another door, pushing it open to reveal a small desk with a white leather chair and a computer. "I'll help you get set up, logged on and save your photo. Then, as I told you before you came, I have to leave before you finish entering your profile. You can leave when you're done. If you want someone to walk you out to your car in the parking garage, the security guard on the first floor can help you."

"Thanks, Leslie. I know I need to get back out there, and I appreciate that you care enough to help me."

"If I didn't think you could be happier, I wouldn't push so much. Give yourself a chance." She hugged Ariana. "Now, let's get this system up and running."

Leslie logged on, brought up the software program, helped Ariana snap a good photo of herself using the webcam and saved it to her profile. Then she stood back and nodded. "The rest is up to you. When you leave, just pull the door to the office closed behind you. It will lock automatically."

"Don't worry about me," Ariana said, waving her away. "I'll do my best."

"You're an amazing woman, and I can't wait to see who BODS comes up with for you." Leslie smiled and left the room, pulling the door closed behind her with a soft snick.

Ariana frowned. She had forgotten to ask what BODS stood for. She could guess the letters "ODS" were for Online Dating Service, but the B?

She shrugged. Next time she saw Leslie, she'd remember to ask. In the meantime, she had a questionnaire to fill out and her life to change.

After she entered the standard information about her age, height and occupation, she started into her preferences, likes and dislikes. This part was harder than she'd anticipated. At one time in her past, she'd been very structured and had liked keeping tight control on everything in her life. She'd worked at a Fortune 500 company, scheduled meetings, worked with others and kept a regimented work and home life.

Until Sam had been diagnosed with pancreatic cancer.

All through his treatments, she'd tried to maintain control of her world, but found the control slipping, slipping, slipping until Sam had died in her arms. She'd felt like a shadow of herself by the time the funeral was over, and she'd run out of leave. Returning to the corporate world had been a disaster.

She hadn't been able to make it to meetings on time, lost focus on her work and hadn't wanted to be there. Within a week of her return, she'd handed in her resignation and wallowed in her grief for a couple more weeks, until she'd gone to see her doctor for anti-depression medication.

Her doctor had asked her to consider grief counseling first. That's when she'd found the Good Grief Club, and met Leslie Lamb, Emma Jacobs, Ava Swan and Fiona McKenzie. They were the ones who'd helped her to regain her balance and encouraged her to learn more about meditation.

Meditation had led her to yoga. Still searching for what she wanted to do with her life, she'd decided to open her own studio to help others find their balance. She'd learned that she couldn't hold onto the past. She couldn't control everything around her, and that was okay.

Now, she sat in front of a computer and tried to think of her preferences in a mate, or in her case, a date.

Someone who didn't take life too seriously. No one comes out of it alive. Someone who lived each day to the fullest like it might be his last. He had to love animals, especially cats, and it would be nice if he was into yoga. Size and shape didn't matter. Although tall and fit wasn't necessarily a good thing. Sam had been tall and fit. It hadn't bought him any extra hours of life. Maybe short and pleasantly plump would be a better choice this time around. A man who liked to eat would be easy to please, and she wanted to learn how to cook.

A guy who didn't live every second dependent on a schedule. He had to be spontaneous, living in the moment, awake to the world around him, not just a narrow lane of existence. Someone who wasn't afraid to stop and smell the roses.

Ariana finished her list of preferences. Before she could change her mind, she saved her profile and exited the software program. She stood, stretched, and was about to head out of the room when a huge crash of thunder shook the building.

The clouds she'd seen through the window, building to the west, must have moved in while she'd been filling out her profile and questionnaire.

As she reached for the doorknob, the lights blinked out, followed by another impressive blast of thunder.

Ariana jumped, her heart beating hard in her chest. She waved her hand in front of her where she thought the doorknob should be. Her fingers brushed against the metal. She wrapped her hand around it, yanked open the door and stepped out into the hallway.

Darkness surrounded her. The only light she could see was a faint red glow at the end of the hallway, possibly in the reception area. Maybe a battery powered exit sign...?

Following the glow, she walked down the hallway, her eyes wide, trying to adjust to the lack of light.

The sound of a door swinging open beside her made her turn. A large dark shape emerged from a room and slammed into her.

She bounced against a muscular chest, the force of impact pushing her backward, off balance. Her back hit the wall on the other side of the hall, and her arms flailed but couldn't help her as she fell hard on her ass.

"Damn!" A deep voice echoed off the walls. "Who's there? Are you all right? Hell, where are you?" The shadowy figure bent in front of her.

Ariana felt a large hand on her leg, patting its way up her thigh to her arm. When knuckles brushed against her breast, she gasped. "I'm okay."

He gripped her arm. "Are you sure? I'm sorry. I didn't see you. Hell, I can't see a damned thing. What the hell happened to the lights?"

"The lightning?" Ariana offered.

"Let me help you up." His hand slid down her arm, sending tingling sensations throughout Ariana's body. When he found her hand, he wrapped his around it and tugged.

She flew to her feet and crashed into the big man's chest, the air knocked from her lungs. At least that's what she told herself. Surely it wasn't the sensation of being held against a muscular man's body that made it difficult for her to breathe. A strange man, at that.

"I thought I was the only one here," she said when she could collect enough air in her lungs to pass it over her vocal cords.

"Me, too," he said. "Are you sure you're all right?"

She nodded then realized he wouldn't see her head move. "I'm sure." She took a step backward, finding it easier to breathe when her breasts weren't smashed up against his chest.

"I was headed out," he said. "Maybe we can find the exit together...?" Still holding her hand, he ran his fingers up to her elbow and held her there.

She liked that his grip helped her find her balance in the darkness. She didn't know him from Adam, but she had an uncanny feeling that she could trust this stranger. "Are you one of Leslie's clients?"

He grunted. "Yeah," he said. "How about you?"

"Just signed up."

"Me, too. Though I'm not yet convinced a computer is the best way to match people."

"You and me both."

He guided her down the hallway, toward the red glow. When they emerged in the reception area, Ariana could see the red glow was indeed a battery powered Exit sign, hanging over the entry door. She looked up at the man guiding her, seeing his face for the first time since they'd bumped into each other.

He was tall compared to her five feet two inches,

almost a head taller than her. He had broad shoulders, which she already knew, having run into them. The red light didn't really tell her what color his hair was, but if she had to guess, by the lightness, it was blond. And she'd bet he had blue eyes to go with that thick blond hair. A shiver of awareness rippled through her.

"We should be able to find our way out of here if we follow the exit signs." The stranger pushed through the door and held it open for Ariana.

Ariana was oddly pleased that he hadn't released her arm and was still escorting her as they left the office. He closed the door snuggly and checked that it was locked before he started toward the elevator.

"Did Leslie talk you into trying out her matchmaking system?" Ariana asked.

"Ha," the man said. "My sister is pushing this agenda. She's convinced it'll be good for me."

Ariana tilted her head. "You don't agree?"

"What do you think about it?" he asked without answering her question.

She smiled in the darkness, glad they'd stepped away from the exit light and he couldn't see her expression. "It could work."

"But?"

"I'm not convinced I'm ready for anything to *work*."

"My sister made me promise to go into it with an open mind."

Ariana chuckled. "And I, of all people, should be following that advice."

"Why of all people?"

"I teach meditation and the art of Zen at my studio to people who have far too much stress in their lives."

"Maybe I should become one of your students," he murmured.

She glanced up at him. "Are you stressed?"

He shrugged. "Only when things get out of control."

They stopped at the elevator.

"The electricity is off," he said. "The elevators won't be working. We'll have to take the stairs down."

"Are you stressed?" she repeated.

"No more than usual," he responded. "Why?"

She could almost hear the frown in his voice. Ariana smiled. "The elevator isn't working. You can't control the fact the electricity is out."

"True. I can't make the electricity come back on," he said. "I *can* control what I do with the knowledge I have." He nodded toward the red light of the exit sign above the door at the end of the hall. "I can take the stairs. I think I can manage twenty flights. I'm still in control, so I'm not stressed."

"What situations cause you stress?" she asked as she walked with him to the stairwell.

"The kind where I'm reliant on other people to make a decision or get work done on time. Sometimes, like the electricity, I can't make them go faster, or get the work done on time. It frustrates me." He opened the door.

She stepped into the stairwell. "And stresses you," she said. "That's where I come in. I can't help you control everything in your life, but I can teach you how to meditate, lessen the stress and let go of the frustration."

"Impossible." Still holding her elbow, he started down the stairs with her.

"It's possible, if you believe. You soon learn that you can't control everything in life. Sometimes, you have to accept that you can't and let go."

He chuckled. "That's where I'd fail miserably as your student. I can't let go."

"Is that why you have difficulties accepting that Leslie's software program might actually choose a good match for you?" she asked. "Because you're not in control of the choosing?"

His hand tightened on her elbow. For a moment he didn't answer. Then he relaxed his hold. "You're probably right."

"In this case, you could let go and let whatever happens, happen."

He snorted. "And here I thought I was uptight about the whole thing because I don't have time and the project I'm working is not going to make the deadline."

"What will happen if you don't make your deadline?"

"I built my reputation on my ability to bring a project in on budget and, most of all, on time. Speaking of the project, I still need to make half a dozen calls tonight and make sure the right supplies are delivered in the morning."

They'd descended fifteen flights by then.

Ariana was enjoying the man's company. She was about to ask his name when the lights flickered and came on. "Well, looks like we can take the elevator the rest of the way down."

"I don't know about you, but I was enjoying the walk," he said, smiling down at her.

"Me, too," she admitted. "Only five more floors to go."

"Might as well walk them," the stranger said.

"Don't you have some calls you need to make?" She tilted her head to the side.

He smiled. "I'm sure cellphone reception in this stairwell is lousy. I'll make those calls later."

"See? You can do it. You can let go of that control. Even if only for a few minutes."

He grunted. "You'll make a convert of me before we reach the bottom."

"I doubt that, but you'll have a start."

"The next thing you'll have me doing is goat yoga and singing 'Kumbaya.'"

"As a matter of fact, I lead yoga classes as well. I'd

be glad to show you some poses. As for the goats, you'll have to bring your own. And, unless you can sing, I'll leave 'Kumbaya' to those with more vocal talent than I possess."

He laughed out loud. "If it makes a difference, I feel more relaxed already."

She smiled up at him. "And here we are. At the bottom." She pushed through the door into the lobby of the office building.

"Will you let me escort you to your car?" the stranger asked.

"I'd appreciate that, as the security guard appears to be busy answering calls." She nodded toward the front desk where a guard had just hung up the phone when another call came through.

They nodded to the guard as they passed and left through the door to the garage, descending one more flight of stairs.

Ariana wished there were more stairs. She wasn't quite ready to leave this man. She liked how relaxed and comfortable he made her feel after how tense she'd been over coming to the BODS headquarters. Here she was talking to a strange man, and it wasn't awkward or difficult at all.

"This is my car," she said as they approached her Audi SQ5, the car her husband had always wanted and had just purchased when he'd gotten his diagnosis.

"Thank you for keeping me company on the tower descent," he said, giving her a little bow.

"Thank you for seeing me safely to my vehicle," she said with a nod. "If you decide you want to come to my meditation class, get a hold of Leslie, she can tell you how to find me."

"What if I want to know how to find you before that?" He took her hand. "I like talking to you."

She smiled. "We've just committed to letting Leslie's system find our matches."

"Didn't you just say I should let go of my stress and the things I can't control?" He raised an eyebrow in challenge.

Ariana wanted to do like he said and let go of that stress and uncertainty. Still… "Leslie is convinced her software will find the one who is right for each of us." She looked up into blue eyes. "We should at least give it a chance."

He nodded. "I get it. You don't want to go out with me."

"I didn't hear you ask."

"If I did?"

She shook her head. "BODS is churning away as we speak, now that the electricity is back on. It could already have found someone perfect for you."

"And you."

She shrugged. "Maybe."

"Will you let me know if it doesn't work out for you?" he asked.

She nodded. "I'd like that."

The man held out his hand. "It's been nice talking with you."

"And with you." She placed her hand in his, and the electric current that raced up her arm excited and frightened her. Ariana could see herself falling for this guy, and she just wasn't ready for that level of intensity. Not yet. She dug her keys out of purse and clicked the unlock button.

The stranger opened the door and held it for her.

She hesitated. "As I probably won't see you again, I just want to say I enjoyed our conversation. More than you'll know." She slipped her hand around the back of his neck and pulled him down to kiss her.

And he did.

Deep, sexy and thorough. She liked the way he tasted and how he held her in his arms. Gentle but commanding.

When he stepped back, she climbed into her car.

He closed her door and watched until she started the car, shifted into drive and pulled out of her parking space.

She'd reached the outer exit when she realized... she hadn't even asked for his name, nor had he asked for hers.

CHAPTER 3

DILLON COULD HAVE KICKED HIMSELF. He'd let his stairwell companion get away before he'd remembered to ask for her name.

Then again, she'd been adamant that they should give BODS a chance. If all else failed, and he didn't like the woman the system chose for him, he could always hit up Leslie for the redhead's name.

He hadn't realized she was a redhead until they'd entered the stairwell with the emergency lights illuminating her long straight hair. And then, it wasn't until the regular lights had come on that he'd noticed she had hazel eyes.

Normally, he would have said he preferred brunettes, but that hair... He found himself wanting to run his hands through it and test to see if it was as soft and silky as it appeared. She'd worn a long, floral skirt with a marigold top cinched at the waist by a gold chain belt. What he liked most were the pointed-toe cowboy boots on her feet. Not true. What he'd like best were her eyes.

Hell, he liked the whole package. Why did he need a system like BODS to find a date? He'd bumped into someone he could see himself going out with, without going through a matchmaking algorithm.

Then again, she wasn't the kind of woman he normally went out with. His usual woman was all the highs: high class, high heels and high maintenance, wearing designer clothes that could fit in a board room as easily as a country club with the wealthiest clients. Yeah, maybe he should wait until BODS found his perfect match. He was curious now to see how his "perfect match" would compare with the redhead.

As he drove out of the garage, rain poured down on his truck, making it difficult to follow the redhead. Not that he would. He had a date with a beer and his brothers at the Firehouse Lounge.

He parked his truck in the parking lot near the bar, dragged in a breath and braced himself for his brothers' ribbing. His only consolation was that they would go through this whole matchmaking scheme soon enough, and he'd get to poke fun at them and make them just as uncomfortable as they would make him this evening.

He was soaked in the downpour by the time he

entered the bar. Ace spotted him from a table in the corner and waved a hand.

As he approached his brothers, all had wide grins splitting their faces.

Ace pushed a mug of beer into his hands. "Drink."

He accepted the offering and tipped it back, drinking half the mug before setting it on the table. "Hit me with your best shots."

"How was it?" Colton asked.

"Not bad. I finished the questionnaire in less than forty-five minutes," Dillon said.

"Then what took you so long to get here?" Brand demanded.

"Electricity went off. I had to make my way down twenty-flights of stairs," he said. No way was he going to tell his brothers that he'd had company all the way down.

"The leading edge of the storm was pretty wicked," Ace said. "We made it here right before it hit."

"Did Leslie say how long it would take to find you a match?" Colton asked.

"No. But she helped me download the phone application." He patted the pocket containing his cellphone. "When it finds a match, it'll notify me with a text. Then I can go online to see who she is."

"Seriously?" Colton leaned toward him. "Show me the app."

Dillon pulled his cellphone from his pocket and

tapped the screen. He pointed at the icon for the BODS system. "If you were that interested, you should have stuck around and filled out your own profile and questionnaire at the same time as I did," he said, though he was glad Colton hadn't. He'd had the redhead to himself all the way down the stairwell.

"What did you put as preferences?" Colton asked. "Your usual brunette ice woman who could have a roomful of corporate executives on their knees begging for their jobs with one killer look?"

Dillon frowned. "I didn't give a hair or eye color preference." He had stated a preference for a tall woman. Now that he had a chance to think about it, he hadn't minded bending down to give his mystery woman a kiss, even though he'd had to bend way down to kiss the redhead. She'd been a good head shorter than him. But he'd liked how petite and feisty, she was.

"A computer shouldn't take long to put two profiles together," Ace said. "I'm surprised you didn't get a match before you left the office."

Except the electricity was off. "The system might have gone down with the power outage."

"Most corporations have their computers on battery backup for just such occasions," Brand pointed out.

"True. So, why haven't you gotten your text with your perfect match?" Colton asked, one eyebrow cocked.

"Maybe the server is down." Dillon lifted his beer and drank.

"Maybe the outage fried your profile, and you need to start all over," Brand suggested.

Dillon didn't want to think about that. Once was enough. If he had to go back, he would just tell Emma and Leslie to forget it.

His cellphone chirped and vibrated, letting him know that he'd received a text message.

His pulse quickened. For a brief moment, he thought it might be his pretty stairwell companion, until he remembered they hadn't exchanged phone numbers.

"Check it out." Colton snatched away his cellphone and brought up his text messages.

"Give me that," Dillon demanded, reaching for his cellphone.

Colton pulled it out of his reach. "It's from BODS," he said with a grin, and then read aloud. "Congratulations, we've found your prefect match. Click on the link to take you to her profile." Colton whooped. "Dillon's got a match."

When Colton tried to duck away from Dillon's reaching hand, Dillon punched him in the arm. "Give it. Unless *you* want to go out with her."

Colton's brow twisted. "No way. BODS matched you with her. You'll have to bite that bullet and go out with her."

"Then give me the damned phone so I can check her out to see if she's anyone I'd be interested in."

Colton tossed the cellphone to Brand.

Dillon glared at Colton and held his hand out to Brand.

Brand gave it to him. "Let's see what you got."

"Not what…" Ace corrected. "Who."

Dillon clicked on the link and a profile came up with a name: Ariana Davis. He frowned. No picture.

"Is she a dog?" Brand asked.

"Show us," Colton urged.

Ace leaned forward. "Yeah, man. Show us."

"Something must be glitchy with the system." Dillon frowned. "It didn't come up with a photo. But I did get a little of her background."

"So, what does she do for a living?" Ace asked.

"It says she's a business owner," Dillon read aloud.

"What else?" Colton asked.

"She not a vegetarian."

"That's good, considering we raise cattle on the ranch," Ace said.

"Can she ride a horse?" Brand asked.

Dillon scrolled through. "She doesn't say."

"Like dogs?" Ace asked.

Dillon shrugged. "She likes animals."

"That could be anything," Brand said. "Monkeys, gerbils, hamsters."

"Cats," Colton added.

"If she likes animals, she'll like dogs and horses. If she doesn't ride, she can learn," Ace said.

"Does she like country music?" Brand wanted to know.

Dillon looked. "Soft rock and big bands from the 40's."

Colton frowned. "How old is she?"

Brand snorted. "Sounds like Grandma."

"Says she's twenty-nine," Dillon said.

"Like I said," Brand gave a knowing nod, "an older woman."

Ace shook his head. "Only a year older than Dillon. Not an issue."

"Are you going to ask her out?" Colton asked.

Dillon thought of the redhead in the stairwell. Before he could ask her out, he had to give BODS a chance. The sooner, the better. "Yes. Might as well get this over with."

"That's the right attitude," Ace said, his voice dripping with sarcasm. "Like marching toward a guillotine."

"You know what I mean," Dillon said. "Do you really think a computer can match two people?"

Ace lifted an eyebrow. "It worked for Emma and Coop. We all know how much they love each other."

"Look, I agreed to do this for Emma. And I will," His eyes narrowed into slits. "But if it doesn't work out, I don't want any crap from the rest of you. Remember, you're all up next."

Colton raised his hands. "I'm not giving you any crap. I know my time's coming, and I'm not anymore pleased about it than you are."

"Why are you all so negative about this dating system?" Ace asked. "You don't have to marry the first person BODS comes up with. Just go on a date. Show Emma you're trying. She'll get over it when it doesn't work out."

"Now, who's the negative one?" Colton crossed his arms over his chest. "You're assuming it won't work out."

"*When* it doesn't work out...*if* it doesn't work out...semantics." Ace sighed. "Just do it to make Emma happy. We gave her enough grief about getting back into the dating scene. She deserves the benefit of the doubt on this BODS thing."

"I'm texting Ariana now," Dillon said. "I'll go out once, but that's all I'm promising."

Colton turned to Brand. "Wanna bet on how this turns out?" He slapped a twenty dollar bill on the table. "Twenty dollars says Dillon marries his match."

Brand's eyes widened. "You're all positive." He reached into his wallet and pulled out two fifties. "I meet your bet and up the ante to one hundred dollars. I'm betting he'll ditch her."

Ace slapped two one hundred dollar bills on the table between them. "Make it two hundred, and I'm betting *she'll* ditch him."

Dill stared at the money on the table. "You guys suck."

As Ariana left the garage and headed home to her house in the suburbs of west Austin, she tried to get the handsome stranger out of her mind. No amount of Zen-anything would shake his image loose.

By the time she got home, she was on the verge of calling Leslie and asking for the man's number.

Instead, she entered her house, lit twenty candles, ran a hot bath with essential oils and sank into water up to her neck. She closed her eyes and pictured a beautiful field of ripened wheat waving in the breeze.

A handsome face and broad shoulders rose up out of the wheat and walked toward her, a sexy grin spreading across his face.

Ariana's eyes popped open, and she sat up straight, splashing water over the edge of the tub. "No, he's not the one. BODS is working on my match." She had to be patient and wait for Leslie's program to sift through the data and connect her to someone truly perfect for her.

A little voice whispered in her ear, *Who could be more perfect than the stairwell stranger?*

Ariana dipped a washcloth in the water, wrung it out and placed it over her eyes. She sank back down in the water and focused on serenity. She was almost there when her cellphone pinged with an incoming text.

She ignored it. The text could wait until she cleansed the tension from her system.

But what if it's BODS sending you the data on your match?

Sitting up again, water sloshed over the edge of the bathtub, as she reached for her cellphone on the bench beside her. She fumbled with the device, her hand wet and slippery with essential oils. When she had the phone steady in her hands, she swiped the screen and read the text.

Congratulations! BODS found your match!

Click here to view your match's profile.

Her heart beat so fast, Ariana felt like it might just leap out of her chest. She clicked the button and waited while the application pulled up the man's profile.

No picture?

Where the picture should have been was a silhouette of a face and a note: *Photo unavailable at this time.*

"Damn." She sighed and scrolled through the personal data. At least she had a name. Dillon Jacobs.

She frowned. Her friend Emma's last name was Jacobs. Could it be one of her four brothers? Jacobs was a pretty common name. Maybe not.

She read more about the man.

He was in construction. That was good. Warmth spread throughout her body and down low in her belly. A man who worked with his hands would know what a woman wanted and know how to get her there.

So far, he intrigued her.

He liked dogs and horses. Another attribute in his favor. Ariana couldn't be with a man who didn't like animals.

He enjoyed fishing, hunting, sports and the outdoors. Ariana shrugged. She had never been fishing, but she was willing to give it a try. Her father had been an accountant, a little nerdy and never into sports or interested in the outdoors, beyond his neatly trimmed yard.

Ariana loved getting outside and going for long walks. It could work.

She drew in a deep breath and let it out slowly. She could go out with Dillon Jacobs. One date wouldn't be too much trouble. Hopefully, he would let her pick the location for the first date. That way she would know what to expect.

So, how did she go about letting him know she was interested? She scrolled down and found a button to push if she wanted to know more.

As she pressed her finger to the screen, another text came through, flashing across her phone.

Ariana, this is Dillon Jacobs. BODS matched us. Want to go out tomorrow?

Her heartbeat fluttered, and then pounded so hard she could barely breathe. As she positioned her hands to respond, the phone slipped and fell into the tub.

"Shit!" she cried, pushed to her feet and fished for her phone. Once she could get her fingers around it, she stepped out of the tub and wrapped the device in a towel.

Please, please, please, still work, she prayed as she dried the phone and looked down at the screen.

Nooooo! Ariana sank to the bathmat on the floor and shook the phone, hoping the water it had ingested would fly free and the phone would miraculously recover.

She tried rebooting it. Nothing.

Rice? Oven? Anything?

She ran naked through her house, dripping on the wood flooring. When she rounded the corner of the hallway and moved into the living room, she slipped and nearly crashed to the floor. A quick hand out to the side caught the wall, and she slowed her pace a little as she hurried to the kitchen.

She pulled out a glass casserole dish, poured uncooked rice into it, laid the phone in the rice and placed it in the oven. The she turned the oven on low and murmured a prayer. A friend had used this technique when she'd dropped her phone in the toilet. Surely bath water with essential oils wouldn't be worse than toilet water.

With her phone in the oven, Ariana raced back to the bathroom, wrapped herself in her bathrobe and wiped up the trail of water from the bathroom to the kitchen before she fell and hurt herself.

When she got back to the kitchen, she pulled the phone out of the oven and tried it again. The damned thing wouldn't even boot.

Ariana stared at the clock on the microwave. It was ten-thirty at night. Would Leslie still be awake? If she was, what could she do? Ariana needed a new phone and soon. Her match would be expecting her to answer his text, in the morning at the latest.

Now, she was beginning to rethink her decision to disconnect her land line. With no phone to make any calls, she couldn't call Leslie, even if she wanted. Nor could she call Emma to ask if one of her brothers was named Dillon.

What about her computer? She could get on social media and look for Dillon Jacobs.

She hurried to her laptop and flipped it open. The battery was dead. Ariana ran with it to her office and plugged it into the charger.

Minutes later, she brought up the logon screen, keyed in her password and googled Dillon Jacobs.

As the screen was coming up, her laptop blinked out, the screen going completely blank.

Ariana squealed. "What the ever-lovin' fuck!" Everything she touched seemed to be blitzing out on her. She didn't have a desktop, having gotten rid of it in her effort to be more minimalistic. With no computer and no phone, she was out of luck. She couldn't even consider calling Leslie for the phone number of the man who'd walked her out of the BODS offices.

Trudging back to her bedroom, Ariana dressed in her night clothes and lay in her bed, staring at the ceiling. Hell, she was afraid to touch the remote for the television. It might break as well.

For a long time, she stared at the texture on the walls, imagining stairwell guy with a quirky smile on his face, laughing at her stress-reducing techniques. Where were they now? They sure as hell hadn't worked when everything had blown way out of her control.

Ariana reminded herself that some things were worth worrying about. Others...well...it just wasn't that important. In the scheme of things, not being able to respond to a text for one night wasn't that big a deal. It wasn't cancer. She'd live through the disappointment and frustration.

After a while, her eyelids drifted closed. Her last thought was not of the text she needed to reply to, but of the big guy she'd met at BODS. What was he doing at the moment? Was he thinking about her at all?

CHAPTER 4

DILLON LAID awake half the night with his cellphone beside him on the pillow, waiting for a response from his BODS match.

By morning, he still hadn't slept worth a damn, so he rose before his alarm, dressed in shorts and running shoes and went for a run. When he got back, he still hadn't received a return text in response to asking Ariana out.

He opened the app and checked her profile. Still no photograph of the woman he hoped to meet that day. He thought about the redhead. Hell, he'd thought more about her than this Ariana woman. He wished he could get on with the BODS date so he could prove they weren't going to fall for each other. Then he would ask the redhead out.

With a construction site to run in downtown Austin, he didn't have time to watch his cellphone for a text. He showered quickly, dressed in jeans and boots and grabbed his hard hat before leaving his downtown condo for the job site.

Though it was Saturday, he expected to see a busy crew working by the time he arrived at eight o'clock in the morning. He'd been paying overtime for the men to show up to work on weekends for over a month now. It was biting into his profits, but he refused to miss the deadline. His reputation as a contractor had been built on his ability to get jobs done on time and within budget. He had contingency funds built in to pay the overtime, so he wasn't too worried about funds, but the timeline was tight, and he wasn't sure how he'd bring it in on the due date.

As he pulled up to the site, he swore beneath his breath.

His crew was sitting around, doing nothing. Only half the people he'd expected had shown up.

He met the foreman, Patrick Sutton, in the portable trailer.

Pat stood with a phone to his ear when Dillon entered. He raised a finger to tell him he'd be a minute. "Okay. But be here as soon as you can make it. We have guys waiting on your work." He ended the call and gave Dillon a tight-lipped look. "Joe Felton didn't show up this morning."

Dillon swore. "What's his excuse now?"

"He spent the night in the ER with his son."

Dillon frowned. "Is the kid all right?"

Pat nodded. "He has an acute ear infection. He was screaming bloody murder while I was on the phone with Joe."

"Why can't his wife take care of the boy?" Dillon asked, irritated that nothing seemed to be going right.

"His wife is expecting their third child. She stayed home with the five year old." The foreman planted his fists on his hips. "They're doing the best they can."

Dillon looked at the ceiling for a second, trying to think. "We need backup. Is there anyone else who can fill in for Joe?"

Pat shook his head. "He's the only one who knows where he left off laying in the plumbing throughout the building. We have to wait for him before we can start closing in walls."

Again, Dillon swore. "What do I have to do to speed up the timeline?"

Pat shrugged. "We're doing all we can. Every construction crew in the city is backlogged with work. It's a good place to be, but not when you need more people to help out on a job. We can't get skilled labor." Patrick's brow dipped lower. "Have you thought of talking with the customer and seeing if they would be all right extending the deadline another two weeks? I think we can wrap everything up by the end of the month."

Dillon grimaced. "I'd rather not."

"I know. You have a reputation to uphold."

"And it gets us jobs others might not win because people know we'll get it done on time," Dillon reminded him.

"We couldn't have counted on having a month of torrential rain slowing us down. Austin doesn't get that kind of rain."

"Until now," Dillon said, his tone flat.

"And you didn't have any control over the metal shortage for beams. Who knew the factory producing them would have a line break down and a union walkout that would last for a couple months?" The foreman raised his eyebrows. "Your customer will understand if you're delayed a couple of weeks."

"I'm not ready to admit defeat," Dillon said, his back stiffening.

The foreman snorted. "You might not be, but some of the guys who've worked for a month straight, without a day off, are ready to walk off the job."

Dillon frowned. "I'm paying a hell of a lot of overtime."

"Hate to break it to you, but money isn't everything." He stepped past Dillon. "Now, if you'll excuse me, I have a site to run on my thirty-third straight day of working."

The foreman left the trailer and slammed the door behind him.

Dillon's gaze followed the man as he stomped toward the waiting crew.

Dillon could do almost every type of job on the site. He'd started working construction when he'd been fifteen and fudged about his age to land a job with a local builder, constructing new homes for some very wealthy clients in Austin. Along the way, he'd run into some of the most famous actors and musicians who'd made Austin their home.

Working with them had helped him see what he'd have to do to gain trust and build a business from scratch. All you had to do was be honest, manage your sub-tiers and get the job done on time and within budget. He'd perfected the budgeting by doing his homework and giving accurate bids. The time aspect of each project always seemed to be the hang-up. Getting crews to show up on time required having them at your disposal and keeping them employed so they'd be there for the next project.

Because he'd started so young, Dillon had learned the business and broke out on his own at the tender age of eighteen. By twenty-seven, he'd grown his business into a multi-million dollar enterprise. What he hadn't made through construction, he'd made through investments. He'd built several speculative buildings in high-traffic areas and sold them for huge profits. Using the profits gained, he'd gotten lucky and invested in the stock market while it was down and watched as the market reached new highs, bringing his portfolio along with it.

He'd made a lot of sacrifices along the way,

working long hours, seven days a week, with little social time. What time off he'd had, he'd used to work on the ranch with his brothers. Which had left little time for him to date.

When the Austin newspaper ran a story about the most eligible bachelors in and around the city, his name, along with his brothers' had been included. Since then, they hadn't been able to date without wondering if the women they met were really interested in them or their money.

Which was why Emma had insisted on Leslie's online dating service.

Again, he had to have time to date. Working seven days a week left him little time to do much else.

And little time for his crew to spend with their families.

He sighed. The men hadn't been off for a weekend in a month. If he didn't give them a break and they walked off the job, he'd be royally screwed.

His mind made up, Dillon left the trailer and walked out to where the foreman was talking to the men. As he walked up behind Patrick, he could feel the animosity in the narrow-eyed stares and the tightly pressed lips. Yeah, they needed a break.

He turned to Patrick. "Pat tells me you're all tired after working a month straight."

The men responded with low grumbling without actually speaking out.

"You know we're behind on this project, but I

think working you into the ground isn't going to make it go faster. When we're tired, we make mistakes. Mistakes can cause even more delays. That being said, it's up to you. You're here now. You can stay and work or take the weekend off."

Immediately, their faces changed from sour to jubilant.

Dillon grinned. "I take it you're opting for the weekend off."

As one, they shouted, "Yes!"

"Be back Monday morning to work hard and smart," Patrick said. "When we get this job done, you'll have more time to spend with your families."

"Will do, boss," one of the men said as he stripped off his helmet and hurried to his truck.

"Got a fishing pole with my name on it waiting for me at home," another said. "Got it for my birthday a week ago and have yet to christen it in the lake." He grinned and ran for his car.

"Thanks, boss," another man said and ran for his vehicle.

Within five minutes, the site was empty of workers and their vehicles, leaving only Patrick and Dillon.

"You want me to stay and line out the work for Monday?" Pat asked.

"No, you need to get home. I'm sure your wife has a long list of chores for you to catch up on." He clapped a hand on Pat's shoulder. "Thanks for keeping me in line."

"You did the right thing," Pat said. "Take a page out of your own book and give yourself the weekend off. You work too hard. It'll make an old man out of you before you hit thirty."

"Is that so?" Dillon grinned. "Then I might just do that. I know some fences that need mending."

"That's not what I meant. Take some time off. Go see a movie, take a lady out to dinner, go enjoy a day at the lake. Destress."

Dillon frowned. "You're the second person in less than twenty-four hours who has urged me to destress."

"Seriously, you need to. You're wound tight." Pat's lip lifted up on one corner. "My wife's been teaching me yoga. We do it in the evening. It helps me shake off the tension."

Dillon looked at his foreman, seeing him as if for the first time. "Yoga?"

Pat frowned. "Yes. Don't knock it until you try it. It's harder than you think but helps you regain balance." Pat nodded. "Now, if you're done with me, I think I'll go clean up and take my wife to that home and garden show she was wanting to go to this weekend."

After Pat left, Dillon walked around the site with a notepad and pen, with the intention of marking all the things that still needed to be fixed. He ended up shoving the pad and pen into his pocket and leaving without make a single note.

If his employees could see how stressed he'd become, he wasn't doing a good job of hiding it. Maybe his redheaded stairwell buddy and his foreman were right. He needed to relax and take some time for himself.

It was close to noon by the time he climbed into his truck and looked down at his cellphone.

A text had come through from his BODS match, Ariana.

His heartbeat quickened as he opened his text messages and read her response.

Hideout Coffee House on Congress at 2:00?

He knew the coffee house. He'd met clients there on a number of occasions. And it wasn't far from the BODS office.

He squared his shoulders and texted back.

See you at 2:00.

There. That should make Emma happy. And coffee was perfect. All he had to do was spend a maximum of thirty minutes sitting with a stranger he knew nothing about, except for what was in her profile, and then he could head to the ranch for a relaxing time mending fences or mucking stalls. Nothing like getting dirty to make things real.

In the meantime, he could visit one of his other sites, wash his truck and get a bite to eat. He was glad he'd let the guys go home early. They'd been working hard. Maybe they could make up the time by working longer days the next few weeks. He'd figure something out, even if he had to get in and do some of the work himself.

Dillon drove by one of his favorite sandwich shops only to discover a line longer than he wanted to stand in. He switched gears and went to the car wash where he cleaned his truck thoroughly and vacuumed the interior. By the time he was finished, he was sweaty. He had just enough time to go to his condo, shower and change into clean jeans and a blue chambray shirt he could wear mucking stalls later. He slipped one of his straw cowboy hats on his head and pulled on work boots.

He figured there was no use setting Ariana's expectations any higher. The match was from a computer software program. Computers couldn't match living, breathing humans who had complex emotions and desires. He spent a lot of his time in similar clothing, though he had a whole wardrobe of nice clothes he wore when he worked with clients. He preferred a good pair of jeans and a T-shirt for most days of the week.

As he climbed into his truck to head to the coffee shop, his cellphone rang. He didn't recognize the phone number, but he answered anyway. "Hello."

"Dillon," a female voice said. "It's Leslie Lamb."

"Hi, Leslie. What can I do for you?"

"I called to apologize."

"For what."

"The electrical outage last night did something to BODS. It's been glitchy all day. That's why it hasn't found your perfect match yet."

He slowed at a red light. "What do you mean it hasn't found my match? I got a text last night from BODS with a name and the profile of a woman. We've arranged a date at a coffee shop."

"Oh, dear," Leslie said. "I'd hoped to catch you before BODS sent out anything. I'm sure your date will be just fine, but don't be discouraged if it isn't. I can't be sure the system functioned properly. Last night's storm did a number on it. I'm going to reload the program from a backup and run it again. In the meantime, I hope you enjoy your date."

"Thank you for letting me know," Dillon said.

"Sorry to inconvenience you. I know how busy you are."

After Leslie ended the call, Dillon sat with his hand on the steering wheel, wondering if he should text Ariana and tell her what had happened and cancel their date. Then again, Leslie was likely calling her now to tell her what she'd just told him. He glanced at the clock on his dash. Five minutes until 2:00. He'd be a jerk to cancel now. She might actually be punctual and already be sitting there, waiting for him to show.

Dillon wasn't keen on the idea of online dating, but if a woman put herself out there, he'd be damned if he stood her up. It took a lot of courage to go on a blind date.

A car honked behind him. The light had turned green.

He pulled forward, still on course for the coffee shop.

Emma didn't have to know about the glitch. He could get the one date he'd promised her out of the way, glitch or no glitch, and she'd get off his back. Thirty minutes. He could do that.

CHAPTER 5

Ariana had planned on being at the coffee shop fifteen minutes early. She'd left her house in plenty of time, but the traffic had played against her. Someone had had a wreck at a major intersection, blocking traffic for twenty-five minutes. She'd been blocked by the vehicles around her, or she would've turned down a side road and found another way to get to the coffee shop.

She'd spent the morning rushing from one place to the next, looking for someone who could fix her cellphone. In the end, she was told the phone was toast. She had to buy a new one. Thankfully, her data card hadn't bit the dust in the fall into the bathtub. She was able to download all of her data from the card to a new one and upload it into the new cellphone. All in time to text Dillon Jacobs a few minutes before noon.

While she was waiting in traffic, she remembered to call Leslie and ask if Dillon Jacobs was Emma's brother.

At first, Leslie didn't answer the phone. The second time she tried to call, she did.

"Online Dating Service, this is Leslie."

"Leslie, Ariana. Are you busy?"

"Oh, sweetie, I'm glad you called. I've been here since midnight, trying to figure out what's wrong with the system."

Ariana watched a tow truck back up to one of the wrecked vehicles ahead. "Something's wrong with BODS?"

"Apparently, the building was struck by lightning last night and suffered a powerful electrical surge. It did something to my server and the software. I can't be sure how much was damaged yet, but it's been glitchy ever since. Did you get a text from BODS with a potential match?"

Ariana stiffened. "As a matter of fact, I did. I'm on my way to meet him now."

"Oh," Leslie paused.

"Should I be worried?"

"No, dear, not worried. I vet all my clients before I allow them to join BODS. It's just..." She cleared her throat. "I'm not sure BODS sent you an accurate match."

Ariana studied the wrecker driver as he loaded the smashed car onto the back of his truck. "Should I call and cancel?" She glanced at her watch. Hell, she was going to be late anyway. Still, if it was Emma's brother, she didn't want to stand him up. Emma was her friend. Friends didn't do that to family of friends. Ariana sighed. She wouldn't do that to anyone. It took a lot of guts for a man to join an online dating service to get a date.

"I don't think you have to cancel. I'm sure you'll have a good time," Leslie said, though she sounded distracted. "But if it doesn't work out, don't be disappointed. I'm going to reload the system from a backup. It'll be up and running by the end of the day, and it'll find you that perfect match."

"Okay. I'll meet him," Ariana said. "Do you think thirty minutes at a coffee shop is enough, if we don't have anything in common?"

"Thirty minutes should be fine. No use spending more time, if you don't hit it off. Frankly, I think in the first fifteen minutes you'll know if you're compatible."

"I can leave at fifteen?"

"Honey, you don't have to go, but unless you both mutually agree to call it off after fifteen minutes, I'd stay for the thirty." Leslie said something to someone in the background. "I have to go. Tag's helping me reload the backup. I'll have my phone if you run into any difficulties."

"Thanks, Leslie."

"I'm sorry about the mix-up. Hopefully, it'll be fixed soon. Bye." Leslie ended the call.

"In the meantime, I have a date with someone who might not be a match for me." Ariana sighed. "Oh, goodie."

The wrecker was just pulling away as her digital clock on the dash blinked 2:00.

And she was going to be late. Well, if he got tired of waiting for her, he'd leave. She could text and let him know she'd gotten tied up in traffic. Feeling a little better about being late for a date that shouldn't have been, Ariana called on her Zen and drove the rest of the way to the coffee shop, parked and hurried inside.

She looked around, realizing they hadn't arranged for a way to identify themselves to each other. If he'd had the same issues with the app as she had, he hadn't gotten a picture of her.

Ariana walked through the place slowly, searching for a man sitting alone. Unfortunately, there were several. She walked toward one man wearing nice trousers and a white polo shirt. He had his cellphone in front of him, keying away with his thumbs. When he looked up, she gave him a tentative smile.

He frowned and looked back down at his cellphone, turning away from her.

If he was her date, he hadn't liked what he saw.

That was depressing and rude.

Ariana chose to believe he wasn't her date and

moved on to the next man. He sat in a booth by himself. His hair was long, pulled back in a man-bun, and he wore a set of headphones. He nodded his head in time to whatever music he was listening to.

She paused in front of his table and cocked an eyebrow, hoping he would take it as, *Are you my date?* Without her having to say it out loud.

He looked up, his eyes narrowed, and he looked from side to side. He pulled one side of the headphones free. "What? Is my music too loud?"

"No. Sorry. I thought you were someone else." She hurried away. The other man who sat in a booth by himself looked up as she neared. He wore a button-down shirt only half buttoned. He had several gold chains around his neck and as many rings on his fingers. He didn't look like he'd ever been on a horse, and his lips curled in a lounge-lizard sort of smile that made the hackles stand up on the back of Ariana's neck.

Nope.

She turned away from him and got in line behind a broad-shouldered man wearing a cowboy hat, waiting for his turn to order a cup of coffee.

The woman in front of him placed her order and moved aside.

"Coffee," he said.

Something about his voice captured Ariana's attention. She leaned forward and caught a whiff of his cologne. She knew that cologne. But from where?

"Would you like whipped cream on top or a sprinkle of cinnamon?" the barista asked.

"No. Just plain and black," he said.

Oh, yes. It came to her as the barista finished ringing up his purchase and he paid. He turned a little too fast and bumped into her. "I'm sorry," he said, touching her arm.

Though she knew who it was even before he turned, Ariana's heart fluttered, and she had to swallow hard to keep from gasping out load. "I'm okay."

He smiled down at her, his brow furrowing as he stared into her eyes. "It's you."

"Yes, it is," she said with a shaky laugh. "And it's you." Wow, she hoped she didn't sound as stupid as she felt.

"How is it we keep running into each other?" he asked.

"I don't know. Just lucky, I guess."

"Ma'am, can I take your order?" The barista waited patiently for Ariana to pull herself together.

"Yes, please," she said, tearing her gaze away from the man in the cowboy hat. "I'd like an English breakfast tea, plain. No flavoring added, please. Just plain tea"

He laughed. "That's the way I like my coffee."

"Your name?" the barista asked, pen in hand, ready to write it on the cup.

"Ariana," she answered.

The tall cowboy blinked then laughed. "You're kidding, right?"

"No, my name is Ariana." She looked at him, her brow dipping. "Is that a problem?"

He held out his hand. "Ariana, I'm Dillon, nice to meet you."

Her eyes widened as she placed her hand in his and felt a charge of electricity run up her am. "You're kidding, right?"

"No, ma'am. Dillon Jacobs," he said, shaking her hand. "I'm your BODS match."

She giggled, then chuckled, then doubled over laughing.

He shook his head, his brow furrowing. "It's funny, but I didn't think it was *that* funny."

"Did you get the same call I got from Leslie?" she asked, wiping the tears from her eyes.

His frown deepened. "I got a call."

"About BODS being glitchy?"

He smiled, and then chuckled. "That's right. We're not even supposed to be matched."

She shrugged. "We don't know that. The system is wonky. We won't know until she gets it back up and running correctly."

"In the meantime, we each have a date with someone who might not be our match."

"Dillon!" the barista called out. "Ariana!"

They collected their drinks, found a table away from everyone else and sat.

59

Dillon drank his black coffee, while Ariana sipped her plain tea.

"Your profile says you're in construction," she said. "You must like working with your hands."

He nodded. "I like to see the fruits of my labors. I couldn't stand to sit behind a desk all day pushing paper."

"I get that." She tilted her head. "But you're dressed like a cowboy, and you also like horses. "Do you get to ride much?"

"Not as much as I used to," he said. "Work keeps me away from the ranch." He looked down at his clothes. "I'd planned on going to the ranch after—"

"Thirty minutes?" she finished, with a wry smile.

"Yeah." His lips twitched. "How did you know?"

"You were going to give me thirty minutes." She chuckled. "That's how many I was going to give you."

He glanced at his watch. "We have another twenty to go. We'd better make good use of it."

She settled back in her chair smiling. "I have a burning question for you."

He leaned back. "Shoot."

"Are you Emma Jacob's brother?"

Dillon grinned. "One of four."

She nodded. "That explains the cowboy hat and horseback riding."

"What about you?" he said. "You're a business owner."

"You already know my story. Zen meditation and yoga instructor." She raised a hand. "That's me."

"It could be we are mismatched, but I'm glad it was you and not a stranger."

She nodded. "I know what you mean. I wasn't keen on the whole idea, but I let Leslie talk me into it. She and my other friends of the Good Grief Club decided I needed to get back into the dating scene."

He tipped his head, his brows rising. "So, you're part of Emma's grief counseling group?"

She nodded. "I don't know what I'd have done without the Good Grief ladies."

"Did all the ladies of that group lose a spouse or fiancé?" he asked.

"Some lost spouses, some lost other loved ones, like a beloved father."

"And you?" he asked softly.

"I lost my husband to cancer," she said, looking down at her cup of cooling tea.

"I'm sorry." He reached across the table and took her hand. "How long had you been together?"

"We were high school sweethearts. We met in ninth grade, dated all through high school and college, married as soon as we graduated, and he died two years ago. Married six years, together fourteen." She looked up. "So, you see, I haven't been too interested in jumping back into the dating scene. I never really dated anyone else."

"Emma was one of BODS' first success stories.

She wanted all her brothers to experience the same success." His lips twisted. "We kind of bullied her into getting back into the dating scene."

"So, she's bullying you to do the same?" Ariana smiled. "All four of you need help?"

"According to Emma."

"But if you're any indication, you shouldn't have any trouble finding a date. You're clean-shaven, smell good and not bad looking."

He grinned. "You think I'm handsome?"

"I didn't say that," she said, her face heating. "I said you're not bad looking." Hell yes, he was handsome. He made her knees weak and sent electric shocks throughout her body when he touched her—like he was doing now. She glanced down at their hands and wondered if he was even aware that he hadn't let go of her. "Point is, you should have girls flocking to you. And if your brothers look like you, they should have the same."

"It hasn't worked that way," he said. "We've been so busy building our careers and taking care of the ranch, we haven't done much dating."

"And you're getting up in years, and she wants you all to be happy."

"Watch it. You're older than I am, based on your profile."

"Does that bother you?" she asked.

"Not at all. I just don't consider twenty-eight and twenty-nine old."

She wrinkled her nose. "For a woman, we're getting close to the cutoff."

"Cutoff?"

"When we hit thirty, it can be more difficult to get pregnant. That family we always wanted but didn't have time for in our twenties might prove elusive."

"You're not old in your thirties."

"It's one of those things that nature decides for us. We have no control."

"That's what fertility treatments are for," Dillon said. "And you can have all your children at once. A veritable litter of children."

Ariana laughed. "You make it sound easy. Some of the women I worked with in the corporate world waited to have children, and now they can't. Their egg supply dried up."

"Is that why you decided to try BODS?" He looked down at his hand still holding hers. "Are you afraid you might be waiting too late to start a family?"

She glanced out the window, trying not to be too affected by his hand holding hers. "Sam and I wanted to have children. We were trying when he was diagnosed with cancer. He fought it for four years before he succumbed. Babies just didn't happen for us. One day, I hope to have a child or two." Ariana smiled up at him. "How about you?"

"I always imagined I'd have kids someday. I guess Emma's right. We're not getting any younger. If we're going to have kids, we need to start working in that direction."

"So, you need a wife...just to have children?" she asked, narrowing her eyes.

"Of course not. Our parents had a really good relationship. They showed us what we should aim for. A partner in life, someone to love and cherish and share all the good and bad that comes along with any union. And they had five children. I liked having brothers and a sister to grow up with. We never lacked for companionship. We were each other's friends," he grinned, "when we weren't beating up on each other. Yeah. I'd like to have kids."

She could picture a little girl with blond hair and blue eyes like her father. Her heart warmed to the image. "You'd make a good father."

"I like to think I would. I'd teach them to take care of cattle, hammer a nail, fish, ride a horse, and so many other things a kid needs to know."

She met his gaze. "Kids need to know all that to be well-adjusted?"

He crossed his arms over his chest. "Of course."

"I never learned to fish or ride a horse," she said softly. "I think I'm pretty well-adjusted."

His eyes widened. "Riding a horse, I can understand. But you've never held a fishing pole?"

"My parents were older, and my father was an accountant. He wasn't much into the outdoors, except when it came to his lawn and flower garden."

Dillon pushed back his chair and rose to his feet.

Ariana frowned. "Are our thirty minutes up?"

"We've actually been here longer than the requisite thirty," he said. "That's not the point. We're leaving."

"That's too bad. I was enjoying talking to you," she said as he hustled her out of the coffee shop.

"Sweetheart, we're going to further your education," he said as he held the door open and waited for her to pass through.

"What do you mean?"

"We're going fishing."

"Does this count as part of our date?" Ariana asked as he led her toward his truck.

"We haven't kissed goodbye yet, so I'd say yes."

Heat rose up her neck into her cheeks at the thought of kissing Dillon. "What about the glitch with the BODS system? The fact that I've never gone fishing and I haven't been on a horse should have flagged me as incompatible with you."

"And I asked for a tall woman. But you don't hear me complaining?" he said with a grin. "I might even change my mind about short women because of you."

Ariana ground to a halt next to the passenger door of a pickup. "What do you have against short women?"

"Nothing. Except I have to bend so far down to steal a kiss." He winked. "Purely gratuitous. No other reason."

She smiled. That was twice he'd mentioned kissing. Was he talking about kissing women in general? Or had he thought about kissing her...in particular?

A shiver of awareness spread throughout her body.

He held the door open for her to climb up inside his truck.

When she hesitated, he waved her forward. "Hop in. We have all the fishing gear we need out at the ranch and a stocked pond to make it easy to catch. And when we're done fishing, I'll take you riding."

"Are you sure? I thought this was a thirty-minute, get-to-know-you kind of date."

"We did most of that last night on twenty flights of stairs," he said. "You also have my profile. And what better place to get to know someone than to be on the water with your line dipping in?"

It all sounded good to Ariana. "I thought you were too busy to date?"

He shrugged. "I ended up giving my crew the weekend off. I don't have to be anywhere until Monday morning. And my foreman said I needed to destress." He held up a hand. "I told him someone else had suggested the same thing. So, let's destress with a little fishing."

"Aren't you afraid Emma will read too much into your spending more than thirty minutes with your glitch date?"

"I don't care what Emma thinks. I feel the call of

the fishing pole. And I've never taught anyone to fish. It'll be good practice for our kid—for when I have a kid someday."

Ariana ducked her head, her chest swelling at his slip. *Our kid.* Those were powerful words, even if they were spoken by mistake. Those two words left her feeling a little dizzy and out of breath. She applied one of her breathing exercises to bring her back to her center, and then looked up with a smile. "The only plans I had for today involved cleaning my bathroom. Fishing sounds much more interesting." She grimaced. "I'll need to swing by and change into something besides this dress."

His gaze swept her from the top of her head to her toes. "Yup. You'll need either jeans or shorts, depending on if you plan on wading in, a top you don't mind getting worm guts on and an old pair of shoes you don't mind getting wet. Oh, and a hat and sunscreen. You know, Emma's got all that at the ranch. She can loan you what you need."

"You sure she won't mind?" Ariana started to climb into the truck, but the handle was too high for her to reach.

"She'll be thrilled I brought a girl home." Dillon gripped her around the waist and lifted her up into the seat.

She turned and smiled down at him. "Thanks. They don't make these trucks for short people." Ariana tilted her head slightly. "I wonder who

BODS will match us with when it's back up and running."

"I don't know, but it was nice not having to face a stranger in that coffee shop." He grinned. "I feel like we've known each other a long time."

"We have." She laughed. "We've known each other for twenty..." she winked and waited for him to finish her sentence.

"Flights. And look, we're already finishing each other's sentences." He closed the door and rounded the front of the truck.

Ariana's gaze followed him, a smile lingering on her lips.

She wasn't so sure BODS had it wrong. Dillon seemed perfect to her.

Her smile faded. She really did wonder who BODS would come up with for her perfect match, round two.

CHAPTER 6

Dillon climbed in behind the wheel and shot a glance across the console at Ariana. She wasn't anything like the woman he'd imagined BODS would match him with. Leslie could be right; the system had some issues. Yet, he couldn't be happier with the mistake.

Like he'd told Ariana, he felt like they were old friends. Their connection in the stairwell of the BODS building had been casual, without the stress of meeting a blind date. They'd had no prior expectations of each other, and they'd met in the dark. Two people who knew nothing about the other, not even what the other looked like. He would always think of her sweet voice and soft curves as his first impression of her.

"Why are you frowning?" he asked.

Her brow smoothed immediately. "Sorry. I was

just thinking that we'll have to go through the uncertainty of another date with a stranger when BODS is fixed and makes our matches."

"Well, stop," he commanded. "I've been told by two people that I need to unwind. Fishing is about the most stress-free activity a person can do."

She sighed. "You're right." Ariana drew in a deep breath and let it out. "I'm on board. Do all your brothers live on the ranch?"

"They do. At least, for now. I'm in the process of designing another house to be built on the ranch and plan on moving into it when it's done. My brothers plan on doing the same, eventually."

"How was it growing up as one of five kids in a family?" she asked. "Was it noisy? Did you get into fights?"

Dillon chuckled. "There was never a dull moment, that's for sure. We learned to ride practically before we learned to walk. Once we were proficient in the saddle, there was no stopping us. We've been all over the ranch at least a thousand times. It's a great place to grow up. What about you? Siblings?"

She shook her head. "None. My folks were older when they married, and I was their only child. I think I grew up before I was ever a kid. My mother taught me how to ride a bicycle, but there weren't any horses in my neighborhood, and my folks kept me close to home."

"Sounds…" he searched for the right word.

"Boring?" She nodded. "It would have been, but I lived all sorts of adventures."

"You did?" He glanced her way.

She stared out the window, a small smile curling her lips.

Dillon was mesmerized by her. The faraway look in her eyes and the way her auburn hair framed her face made him want to reach out and touch her cheek.

Ariana lifted her chin. "I did have adventures, through the books I read. I escaped to faraway lands, even planets, fought battles and won and fell in love at least a thousand times." She gave him a shy smile. "To me, books were far more interesting than my life."

"That's kind of sad," he said.

"I didn't think so. I had a very dear friend who liked to read as much as I did. We shared a love of fantasy and science fiction from grade school through college." She stared out the window at the road ahead as if she had gone back to a different time. A sad time.

"This friend..." he said quietly, "was it your husband?"

She nodded. "I married my best friend. And as I mentioned, he died of pancreatic cancer."

"That must have been hard. You were together for a long time."

She nodded. "Half my life. Losing him left a huge

hole. I had to learn who I was all over again. So, you see, an online dating service was a big step."

"And the service didn't get it right, matching you and me." He shook his head. "The last book I read was nonfiction. I think it was how to rebuild a tractor engine or maybe the training manual for a computer-aided design program. I haven't read fiction since grade school."

"You should give it a try again. It's very relaxing," she said. "Well, if you're not in a battle scene about to be run through with a sword." She winked. "No, I didn't grow up with siblings to play with, but I wasn't lonely, and I learned a lot through reading."

Ariana's sad face made Dillon want to cheer her up. He couldn't bring back her dead husband, but he could look for ways to make her smile. Because when she smiled, the air around her seemed to light up. He liked that. A lot.

As they drove out to the ranch, Dillon told Ariana some of the trouble he and his brothers and sister had gotten into living on the ranch.

By the time they arrived, she was laughing and smiling again.

When he pulled up in front of the ranch house, Ace came out on the porch. Colton rounded the side of the building and Brand pushed to his feet from his seat in a rocking chair.

"Sorry, I didn't expect you'd have to run the

gauntlet of my brothers," Dillon said, shifting into park. "I thought they'd be out working still."

"It's okay. I'd like to meet them. I feel like I know them already."

"Oh," he leaned toward her, "about that story I told you about skinny dipping in the creek...?" He shook his head. "Don't tell them that was me who hid their clothes. They still don't know who did it."

She pressed her lips together. "Your secret is safe with me."

He got out of the truck and came around to help her down. He'd always gone out with taller women, but he found that he liked how petite she was. It gave him an excuse to put his hands around her waist to help her down. Which he did.

When her feet touched the ground, he found he didn't want to let go.

"Dillon, who've you got with you?" Ace asked.

He held out his hand to Ariana. "Come on, I'll introduce you to my brothers."

Ariana put her hand in his and let him lead her up the steps to the porch.

Starting with the oldest brother, he went down the line. "Ace, this is Ariana Davis. Ariana, my oldest brother, Ace."

He took her hand in his. "Nice to meet you, Ariana."

Brand stepped up. "I'm Brand." He shook her

hand and tilted his head. "You're not like the usual women Dillon dates."

Dillon cringed.

"Dumbass." Ace jabbed an elbow into Brand's side. "You don't say that to a woman." To Ariana, he aimed a crooked smile. "That you're not like the usual woman Dillon goes out with is actually a good thing. Don't let this knucklehead make you feel bad."

"It was a compliment," Brand grumbled, rubbing his ribs.

"And this is Colton," Dillon said, ready to get past his brothers and out to the pond, alone with Ariana.

Colton grinned. "A redhead." He took her hand in his. "Is it true that it's good luck to rub your hand over a redhead's hair?"

Dillon glared at his brother. "Don't even think about it."

His brother's brows shot up. "What? You didn't think I was going to actually do it, did you?"

"I wouldn't put anything past you." Dillon pushed past his brothers and headed for the door with his hand at the small of Ariana's back. "Is Emma here?"

"Did I hear my name?" Emma pushed through the screen door, the smile on her face turning upside down. "Ariana? What are you doing here?"

Ariana lifted her hands, palms up. "BODS matched me with Dillon."

"You're kidding, right?" Emma's glance shot to Dillon. "Seriously?"

He nodded. "Got the text last night, made arrangements to meet this afternoon, and then Leslie called to say the computer system was damaged during the lightning storm last night. By the time she called to let us know, we were already on our way to our meeting location."

Emma's brow wrinkled. "Let me get this straight. BODS didn't work right when it matched you two?"

"That's sums it up," Ariana said.

Emma frowned. "Then why are you two here?"

Dillon grinned. "We figured we might as well make a day of it. I'm taking Ariana fishing, and then we're going to ride horses."

Emma's frown deepened as she turned to Ariana. "I didn't know you like to fish."

Ariana shrugged. "I don't know if I like it, either. I've never been."

"Since she's never been fishing and she's never been on a horse, I thought I'd give her the consolation prize of a free lesson in how to bait a hook and cast a line. When she's mastered that, I'm going to teach her how to ride."

"Okay." Emma reached out and hugged Ariana. "I'm really glad you're getting out. It's about time."

Ariana hugged her back. "You, Fiona and Leslie inspire me to get out of my comfort zone."

Emma grimaced. "Being with any one of my brothers will put you out of your comfort zone quickly." She pointed a finger at Dillon. "You better treat my friend right. No minnows down her britches or worms in her boots."

Ariana's eyes widened. "He's done that before?"

Emma crossed her arms over her chest. "Yes, he has."

Dillon chuckled. "I don't think I've seen you move that fast since." He hooked Ariana's arm. "I promise not to put a minnow in your drawers. Which reminds me." He turned to his sister. "Emma...?"

"Ariana's not dressed for fishing." Emma disengaged her brother's arm from Ariana's and led her toward the staircase. "Come with me. I'll find you some of my old clothes to wear. They might be big on you, but better that than ruin your pretty skirt."

"Thank you," Ariana said. "I don't want to be a bother."

Emma huffed. "You're getting my brother to take a day off. You're a godsend."

Dillon frowned. "I had already decided to take the day off." Well, he'd decided to give the project the day off, anyway. Mucking stalls and fixing fences wasn't like real work. Okay, so it was.

He watched as Emma and Ariana climbed the stairs and disappeared into Emma's room.

Ace draped an arm over Dillon's shoulders. "She's never been fishing?"

Dillon stiffened. "No. So?"

Ace chuckled. "You like the woman?"

He shrugged, not wanting to give anything away

to his brothers. It was too soon in his relationship with Ariana. A relationship that should never have been, according to Leslie and BODS. "She's nice."

"And a redhead." Colton stepped through the door. "You know what they say about redheads."

"It's not good luck to rub their heads," Brand said, entering after Colton. "That's bald men."

"It's not bald men," Ace said. "It's leprechauns."

"It's all three," Emma called out from the doorway to her room. "Seriously, look it up on the internet." She slammed her door.

Dillon grinned. "I think she's right."

"Whatever." Colton shot a glance up the staircase. "Ariana's not who I pictured you with."

His back stiffening, Dillon turned to his brother. "What do you mean?"

"She's short," Colton said.

"Petite," Dillon corrected. "And I like that."

"You've never dated a *petite* woman," Brand said.

"That's right," Ace said. "Most of your women are a lot taller."

"They're not *my* women. And size doesn't matter."

"And you say she's never been fishing?" Colton asked. "Or horseback riding?"

"Neither."

Brand shook his head. "How's she gonna fit in on a ranch?"

"Who said she needed to fit in? It's not like I'm

going to spend a lifetime with her. She's here for the day. That's all."

"Uh huh," Ace said. "She might not even make it that long. Ranch life isn't for everybody."

"She'll do fine." Dillon had had some of the same doubts, but he wouldn't let his brothers know of them.

"Need me to show her how to cast a line?" Ace waggled his eyebrows.

"Hell, no," Dillon said.

"I haven't been fishing in a while," Brand said. "Might just have to go dip my line."

"Me, too," Colton said. "I'll go get my rod." He turned toward the back door.

"Stop." Dillon clenched his fist. "No one else needs to get their rod or dip their line. I'm taking Ariana fishing. Just the two of us."

"Are you really going fishing?" Colton turned back, his eyebrow cocked. "Or do you need to be alone for an entirely different reason?"

Dillon closed his eyes and clamped his lips tightly together. "Why do I bother arguing with you?"

"Because you know you'll never win, but you're an optimist who believes someday you will," Ace said with a grin. "They're just yanking your chain. Aren't you?" He stared hard at Brand and Colton.

"Yeah," Brand said. "Yanking."

"If one of you shows up, I'll kick your ass from

here to tomorrow," Dillon warned. "I should have known better than to bring Ariana here."

"Lighten up," Ace said. "Your woman is ready to go fishing." He gripped Dillon's shoulders and turned him toward the staircase.

Ariana stood at the top, dressed in a pair of denim overalls, gum boots and one of Emma's old T-shirts. She'd braided her hair into two long plaits hanging down behind her ears. On her head, she wore a wide-brimmed straw hat.

"Hello, Orphan Annie," Colton said.

"Howdy Doody," Brand corrected. "She looks like those old film clips of Howdy Doody."

Ariana spun back toward Emma's bedroom.

Emma caught her shoulders. "Don't let them make you self-conscious. You're going fishing, not to a fashion show."

"I know. I know," Ariana grumbled and turned toward the stairs. "Fishing."

"You look great," Dillon said. "These yahoos are just being jerks."

Ariana descended the staircase, holding onto the railing. "The boots are a little big, but Emma gave me three pairs of socks to fill the gap." As she neared the bottom, her toe caught on a step, and she pitched forward.

Dillon rushed forward, catching her in his arms.

"And it's Dillon for the save!" Colton cried out.

Ace, Colton and Brand all clapped.

Muttering beneath his breath, Dillon set Ariana upright. "Those boots are huge on you."

"I should have stopped at my house for shoes," she said, her gaze falling away. "It was nice of Emma to loan me these."

"It was all I had that she could get wet," Emma said as she came down the stairs. "She has really tiny feet."

"They'll be fine. Don't worry. Once we get out there, it won't matter." He slipped a protective arm around Ariana's waist and led her to the door, calling out over his shoulder. "The two of us are going fishing. Emphasis on two."

"Gotcha," Ace said. "I'll make sure Brand and Colton have stalls to clean."

Dillon wouldn't hold his breath. His brothers loved playing jokes on each other. He usually got in the thick of them. Just not this time.

He didn't want Ariana to regret going fishing with him. He liked to think she might go with him again in the future.

CHAPTER 7

ARIANA DIDN'T MISS the irony of her situation as she stepped into the little jon boat and settled on the hard metal bench seat. She'd never been fishing or riding. For that matter, she'd never been on a real, working ranch. And she was about to be launched out into the water. A fish out of water, in the water.

"Here, put this on." Dillon sat across from her and handed her a bright orange life jacket.

She hooked it around her neck and fumbled with the buckle.

He brushed her hands away and wrapped the strap around her waist, leaning in close enough she could smell his cologne.

Ariana inhaled deeply, liking that scent a little too much.

When he brought the strap back around to her

front, he smiled into her eyes as he clipped the buckle. "There. Just in case we capsize."

"I do know how to swim," she said.

"Yeah, but you're weighed down by clothes that are two sizes too big for you." He sat back on his bench, grabbed a paddle and pushed the boat away from the shore.

"You're not wearing a life vest," Ariana pointed out.

"I have one here," he said, pointing to the vest on the floor of the skiff.

"Couldn't we have fished from the shore?" she asked.

"We could have, but the bigger fish are in the deeper water. I have hope we can eat what we catch for dinner."

She cringed. "Are you going to teach me how to clean and cook the fish, as well as catch them?"

He laughed. "I take it by the look on your face, you're not ready for the cleaning part."

Ariana shook her head. "I'm not even sure I'm ready for baiting the hook."

"We'll start with something simple. A worm."

She nodded her head. "Okay."

The pond had appeared fairly small when they'd walked up to the edge. But now that they were out in the middle of it, it looked more like a vast lake. Ariana knew how to swim, but it had been a few years since she'd been in a pool. And it was a long way from the boat to the shore. She tested the straps on the vest, cinching them a little tighter.

They were two-thirds of the way across the pond when Dillon stopped paddling and let the boat drift. He opened a tackle box and pulled out a round white and red thing. He attached it to the fishing line on one of the poles, and then attached a line with a hook on the end.

"You can use this pole. Hold it while I prepare mine." He handed the pole to her. "Careful not to catch your skin on the hook."

Ariana appreciated that he was patient with her. She really had no idea how to catch a fish. She understood the concept of luring a fish with something it liked to eat, but actually catching one and reeling it in…? Not so much.

Once he had his hook and round red and white thing attached, he dug into the can they'd brought that was full of the worms they'd dug out of the pile of horse manure and straw behind the barn. He brought up a worm and threaded it onto the hook. "Watch closely, because you'll be doing this."

"Doesn't that hurt the worm?" she asked.

"No," he said. "Besides, the worm is about to be eaten by a fish, if we're lucky." He dipped his fingers in the water to rinse off the worm guts and horse manure. Then he flipped the metal ring over and, with his thumb on the line, he cast the line and worm away from the boat. "Think you can do that?"

"Maybe."

He dug out a worm and handed it to her. "Let's see you do it."

She struggled to get the worm on the hook, wincing as she pierced the worm's body, feeling sorry for it. The worm wiggled like it was in horrible pain. Arianna almost gave up halfway through the process. But she refused to be the city girl who couldn't fish because she was too squeamish. Once she had the worm on the hook, she flipped the metal ring like Dillon had, but forgot to put her thumb on the line. The hook and worm dropped into the bottom of the boat. "Oops. I don't think that was supposed to happen."

"It's okay. Here…" He reached across, took the pole from her and reeled in the excess line. "I'm coming across to sit beside you."

Very carefully, he moved across the short space between them, rocking the boat as he did.

Ariana held onto the bench seat with both hands, glad she had on the life vest.

Dillon settled on the seat beside her and wrapped his arms around her. "Hold the handle here." He placed her left hand below the reel. "Now, flip this metal ring over the top, while holding your thumb on the line." He pressed her thumb on the line and flipped the ring. "See? It doesn't go anywhere when

you hold it like that. Now, you bring it back like this."
He leaned back, his hands around hers, his arms
surrounding her making her body light up like
Fourth of July fireworks, and he flicked the end of
the rod, saying, "Let your thumb off."

She moved her thumb and the line flew out over
the water, the bobber landing with a plop, the hook
with the worm on the end, sinking beneath the
surface.

"Now, you turn the handle once to set the line."

Ariana turned the handle, hearing a click as
she did.

"Good," he said, still holding her in his arms.
"Think you can manage it from here? Or do you
want me to help you reel it in?"

"If you don't mind, I'd like you to take me through
reeling it in at least once before you turn me loose,"
she said. And she didn't want him to move from
where he sat, holding her in his arms with her back
pressed to his chest.

Who knew fishing could be so sexy?

The bobber dipped beneath the surface.

"Is that supposed to happen?" she asked.

"Yes, ma'am. That means the fish are hitting the
bait. Wait until the bobber sinks below the surface.
Then we'll pull up sharply to set the hook in the fish's
mouth. And yes, it hurts the fish, but we're going to
eat the fish later, anyway."

"You really are going to be good with kids, someday," she said.

The bobber sank below the surface.

"Give it a little jerk," he said, wrapping his hands around hers. He pulled back the rod sharply.

Ariana could feel the tug at the other end. "I have a fish!"

"Yes, you do. Now, reel it in."

She turned the knob slowly.

"Go faster. Sometimes, they're only snagged and can get off easily. Bring it in. I'll get the net for when it gets close enough."

She turned the knob faster and faster, getting a cramp in her hand as she did.

Soon, the bobber popped up out of the water, and Ariana could see the silvery shadow sliding beneath the surface. "I see it!" she cried.

"Hold steady while I scoop it out of the water."

He leaned close to the edge. The skiff dipped down.

Ariana stopped reeling and leaned the opposite direction.

"Pull the pole up so I can get under the fish," Dillon said.

She did as he said, yanking it up a little too fast.

The fish flew out of the water, smacked Dillon in the face and landed on Ariana's lap.

She squealed and lunged away from the flopping fish and toward Dillon who was leaning over the rim of the boat.

With both of them going the same direction, the skiff flipped, dumping the Ariana, Dillon and the fish into the water.

The boat crashed over on top of them, conking Dillon on the head. He went under, beneath the overturned boat.

"Dillon!" Ariana reached beneath the surface, the pond water terrifying in the darkness.

She didn't feel anything at first, then her hand touched something solid. A sob rose up her throat as she dug her fingers into a shirt and pulled Dillon toward her. His head came up beside her in the gap between the boat and the water.

"Dillon!" she said. "Talk to me. Please, talk to me."

She held his head above the water, glad for her life vest. Had his lungs filled with pond water? Was he breathing? Ariana leaned close to his mouth and nose and listened and felt for breaths.

When she didn't feel anything but the pounding of her pulse against her eardrums, she turned him around, slipped her arms around his middle and gave him the Heimlich hug, hoping that would expel any water from his throat and lungs. She did it twice, and then turned him again.

She'd taken an advanced life-saving course prior to opening her Zen studio in case one of her clients had a heart attack. None of that course of instruction had covered how to perform CPR on someone in the water.

She cupped his cheeks in her palms and pinched his nose at the same time. Then she pressed her lips to his and blew air into his mouth. Taking in another breath, she breathed into him again. "Come on, Dillon, wake up!"

On the third breath, he jerked, grabbed her around the waist and drew in a sharp breath.

"Dillon," she said, tears running down her cheeks. "You had me so scared."

Floating in the water, in the darkness of the overturned boat, she sobbed. "So scared."

"Ari?" He reached above him and grabbed hold of the metal bench seat. "What happened?" He let go of her and raised his hand to his head. "Ouch."

She didn't let go of him, clinging to his shirt, afraid that if she let go, he'd sink beneath the surface again, and she wouldn't be able to find him. "The boat tipped over and hit you in the head." She swallowed hard on a sob. "The fish got away."

"The fish?" His body shook.

"Dillon?"

"The fish?" he gasped.

"I'm sorry. I don't know what happened to it when the boat flipped."

He burst out laughing and coughing. "We nearly drowned, and you're worried I'd be disappointed about the fish?" He pulled her close with one arm. "You're something else."

"I think BODS had it right," Ariana said mournfully. "I'm not the match for you. I can't even stay in a boat and fish. I'm so sorry." She reached for the side of the boat and tried to duck beneath it. Her life vest wouldn't let her go deep enough to slip beneath the rim. "Damn it!"

"Hey," Dillon said softly. "We should have started out on the shore until you got used to how fish behave. That was my fault."

"I'm twenty-nine years old. I should have learned to fish by now."

"No, really. I think it's great that you don't know how. It means I get to teach you."

"I nearly killed you." She was glad he couldn't see her in the dark, all wet like a street rat in the rain with red-rimmed eyes. "You should probably take me home."

"Come here," he said, drawing her into the curve of his arm again. "We're okay. You're okay. And we got to go for a swim." He pressed his lips against her forehead.

Ariana stilled, her breath hitching in her throat as his mouth moved down her cheek and found the corner of hers.

"You saved my life," he said. "Thank you." Then his lips covered hers, wet and all, and he kissed her as if savoring every second their lips blended together.

His arm tightened around her as he held her against him.

Though she was glad for the life vest, she wished

it was gone so that she could feel his heart beating against her breasts.

A boot slipped off her foot.

"Damn it!" she murmured against his mouth.

He laughed. "Not the response I expected after that. What's wrong?"

"One of Emma's boots just drifted to the bottom of the pond. Now I owe her a pair of boots. I hope these weren't her favorites."

He laughed and pulled her close. "What say we get out from under this boat."

"I can't. The vest won't let me go under."

"Thank goodness," he said. "It's doing the job it was designed to do. I can push you under long enough to get you to the other side."

"Okay." She drew in a deep breath. "I'm ready."

Dillon pushed down on her vest and shoved her beneath the rim of the boat.

Ariana bobbed to the surface on the other side, gasped in air and spun, looking for Dillon.

When his head surfaced, she let go of the breath she'd been holding and swam toward him.

He held onto her with one hand and the boat with the other. "You all right?"

She nodded. "Now that you're here."

"I wouldn't let anything happen to you," he said.

"I wasn't worried about me. I was worried you wouldn't come out from under that boat." She drew in a deep breath and let it out, turned and looked toward the shore. "I guess we'd better start swimming." Ariana took his hand. "I'd feel better if you held onto my life vest."

He nodded. "I can do that as long as it doesn't drag you down."

"It won't," she said. "Ready?"

He nodded and started swimming, using the sidestroke, so that he could hold onto her and swim at the same time.

Ariana kicked, keeping pace with him. They moved so slowly through the water, she thought they'd never get to the shore. She didn't complain when her legs got tired. She had the flotation device, he didn't.

When they finally reached the shore, she crawled up onto the bank and lay for a moment beside him.

"I have got to swim more often," he said, rolling over onto his back. "That uses entirely different muscles than riding or jogging."

Ariana pushed to a sitting position and fumbled with the buckles on the vest.

Dillon sat up. "Let me"

"I'm not completely helpless," she said. "I'm really good at yoga and meditation. And I was an excellent business analyst when I worked in the corporate field." She sighed and let him deal with the hard plastic clip. "Fine, you do it. I'm just not cut out for ranch life."

"I wouldn't consider fishing necessarily ranch

life," he said. "You might be really good at horseback riding."

She shook her head. "After what we just went through, I'll take a rain check. One round of humiliation is all I can handle in a day."

Dillon pushed to his feet, extended a hand and pulled her up into his arms. "I don't see it that way."

"How else could you see it? Our fishing date was an unqualified disaster." She rested her hands on his chest. "The only good thing that came of it was…" She stopped before she blurted out the truth.

His head dipped until his lips hovered over hers. "The kiss?"

Her gaze whipped to his eyes, and then down to his mouth. "Yes."

"At least we got one thing right." And then he kissed her, without a life vest or cool pond water between them.

Ariana melted into his body, her arms sliding across his muscular chest to lace behind the back of his neck. She rose up on her toes, eager to be even closer.

When he traced the seam of her lips, she opened to him, meeting his tongue halfway with her own.

She clung to his wet body. Nothing seemed to matter but how his mouth felt on hers.

When at last he straightened, she sank down on her feet, remembering she was wearing only one boot now. "We'd better be getting back to the house before they come looking for us."

"I'm surprised my brothers didn't come out to heckle us." He shook his head. "The one time we could have used their assistance." He looped his arm around her waist. "I'll help you to the truck. Just lean on me."

She did, loving how solid and strong he was. She'd lived on her own now for two years since her husband had died, learning how to be comfortable in her own right. Alone. But it felt good to lean on someone else for a while. Even if it was only for a few minutes, and only because she'd lost a boot in the pond. When she stumbled once, he tightened his hold around her waist. The second time she stumbled, he scooped her up into his arms and carried her the rest of the way to the truck. "I'm fine," she said. "It's just that the boot is full of water and too big."

"All the more reason to let me carry you. We'll get there faster, and you can take off that waterlogged boot." He didn't put her down, but carried her all the way to his truck, where he set her down on the front passenger seat.

"But I'm all wet."

"So am I," he said. "The seats are leather. They'll dry." He climbed into the driver's seat and headed back to the ranch house.

When they arrived, his brothers came out on the back porch. Ace carried a tray of raw steaks and was headed for the grill. Colton and Brand each had a beer in their hands.

"Where's your catch?" Colton asked as Dillon dropped down out of the truck.

Brand's mouth curved in a grin when he saw the condition of Dillon and Ariana's clothing. "Did you decide to swim instead of fish?"

"As a matter of fact, we did." Dillon carried Ariana up to the porch before setting her on her feet.

"Lose a boot?" Colton asked.

"I did," Ariana said, heat rising up her neck into her cheeks. "I'm afraid I capsized the boat."

"Is that how your got the knot on your forehead," Ace asked Dillon.

Dillon pressed his fingers to the bump. "The boat flipped. I took a hit, but we're both fine. Oh…and the fish got away."

"And I was looking forward to fish for dinner," Colton said.

"The hell you were," Ace said. "You were the one who wanted steak tonight."

"He wants steak every night," Emma said as she came through the door carrying at tray filled with corn on the cob, each wrapped individually in foil. When she saw Ariana, still completely wet and missing a boot, she shoved the tray of cobs into Brand's hands and rushed forward. "I thought you two were going to fish, not swim."

"They flipped the boat on the pond," Colton said

"That's right," Dillon said, his words a little terse. "We flipped the boat. Now, if you'll excuse us, we need to get cleaned up and into dry clothes."

He touched a hand to the small of Ariana's back.

"You can use my room," Emma said. "Your clothes are still there. You can find freshly laundered underwear in the top drawer of my dresser."

"Thank you." Ariana gave Emma a weak smile. "I'm so sorry about the boot."

Emma's brow twisted. "What happened to the boot?"

"It's at the bottom of the pond."

Emma shook her head. "I'm just glad you two weren't hurt too badly." She pushed the hair off Dillon's forehead. "I'll get you an icepack for that lump. Do you need to see a doctor for a possible concussion?"

He shook his head. "I'm fine. I just want a steak and a beer."

"Go," his sister said. "Get your shower in the master bathroom. I'll take Ariana up."

"You going to be all right?" Dillon asked Ariana.

Heat filled her cheeks at his concern. "I'll be fine."

"Then I'll see you in a few. You might want to tell Emma how you like your steak. She'll let Ace know."

"Medium," Ariana said as she slipped out of the remaining waterlogged boot.

"Noted," Emma replied with a grin.

Dillon headed for the master bedroom to shower, leaving Ariana with Emma.

Emma turned to Ariana. "Did you get hit when the boat flipped?"

"No," Ariana said. "But I'm afraid Leslie was right. BODS is jacked up. I couldn't possibly be the right match for your brother." She trudged up the stairs to Emma's bedroom.

"Why do you say that?" Emma asked, going to the dresser and pulling out clean undergarments. "You two seem to be getting on pretty well, considering you fell into the pond."

"That's just it. I'm not cut out for life in the outdoors. Dillon is a natural. I made our little fishing trip an utter disaster." Ariana's shoulders sank. "It was my fault the boat flipped and hit Dillon in the head." She reached for Emma's hands. "He could have died."

"He said you saved his life, Ariana," Emma squeezed her hands. "He doesn't seem to be in a rush to get you home. Stick around and see where it goes."

"I like him," Ariana said. "I just don't think I could get into a relationship that's doomed from the start. We aren't suited for each other. He needs more of a granola girl."

Emma laughed. "A granola girl?"

"You know, one who eats healthy food, lives, breathes and speaks outdoors. I didn't even know how to put a worm on a hook."

"But you did it today, didn't you?" Emma asked. "Or did my brother do it for you?"

Ariana smiled. "I actually did."

Emma's face brightened. "See? There's hope. And maybe, next time you fish, you can fish from the shore instead of the boat. Speaking of the boat, is it still out there upside down?"

Ariana grimaced. "Yes."

"My brothers will retrieve it tomorrow. They'll love the chance to play in the pond." Emma grinned. "If Coop stays the night, we might all go in the pond to retrieve the boat tomorrow. So, you see, it's not such a disaster."

"I almost caught a fish," Ariana said with a smile.

"It's too bad you didn't get to bring it home to show it off." Emma walked to the door. "Don't be too hard on yourself, Ariana. You're new to ranches and the great outdoors. Give it a chance. You might learn to love it as much as we do."

Ariana gave her friend a tentative smile. "Thank you, Emma. For believing in me."

"I wouldn't encourage you, if I didn't think you were right for my brother. But I've known you for a couple years now, and I know you have a good heart and aren't afraid to try new things. You wouldn't have built a terrific Zen studio otherwise. I also know my brother. He wouldn't have brought you home, if he hadn't seen something special in you. He's never brought home one of his other women."

Her eyes widening, Ariana asked, "Were there many other women?"

Emma grinned. "When he was younger, the ladies would follow him everywhere, except out here to the ranch. They didn't have the code to the electric gate, or they might have camped out in the yard, just for a chance to see Dillon. Lately, he's been working too hard. He needs to learn how to balance work life with relaxation. I hope you can help him with that."

"I'd love to have him attend one of my yoga classes," Ariana said wistfully.

"Ask him," Emma said. "He'd tell me to go to hell. With you...he'll probably say yes."

Ariana stepped across the hallway with her stack of clothes.

When she'd climbed out of the pond beside Dillon, she'd been sure it was the end of their date and any chance at future dates.

After he'd carried her up to the truck, and then kissed her before they'd left the pond, she wasn't so sure the date was over.

She would wait and see if he asked her out again. What would it hurt to go out with him again, even if the computer system had made an error putting their profiles together? If nothing else, Ariana was getting a real-life adventure instead of a fictional one through the pages of a good book.

She hurried through the shower, anxious to see

Dillon again. He still had to take her back to Austin. Would he try to kiss her again?

Man, oh man, she hoped he would.

CHAPTER 8

DILLON HURRIED through his shower and shaved, just because, then slapped on some aftershave. He dressed in the nice trousers and polo shirts he reserved for meetings with clients and his best pair of cowboy boots.

As soon as he stepped out of his bedroom, he knew he'd take a brutal ribbing from his brothers over trying to impress Ariana. Well, to hell with them. He liked her. He reasoned with himself that he respected her and wanted her to feel comfortable and not overdressed in her pretty skirt. He checked his reflection in the mirror. It was a far cry better than when he'd dressed for the meeting at the coffee shop.

The events of the day had gone a lot different than he'd expected. Even with tipping over in the boat, he'd enjoyed being with Ariana. She had a fresh outlook on things he'd taken for granted. He liked that she was game to try something new. She'd gone from a corporate job to turning her grief counseling suggestions into a business she was good at. And a city girl giving fishing a try...well, they'd have to work on that. Plus, he had yet to teach her how to ride a horse.

He slowed as he reached the stairs, pausing in front of Emma's bedroom door. He wanted to knock and see if she was ready to go down but didn't want to rush her. At the same time, he wanted her to hurry so that he could see her again.

He'd never been that anxious to see a woman again. Most dates he'd been on over the past couple of years had ended up in bed. Afterward, he hadn't called the woman to arrange a second date. He just hadn't been that interested.

With Ariana, he wanted the day to continue and was already planning additional dates where they could visit local wineries, ride horses on the ranch and even try fishing again...from the shore. He'd even buy her a pair of boots that fit, if she'd let him.

Dillon headed down the stairs, passed through the kitchen for a beer and walked out onto the porch where his brothers, sister and her husband Coop were drinking beer and grilling steak, corn and potatoes.

"I take it we're going swimming tomorrow," Colton said.

Dillon nodded, twisting the top off the bottle. "I

could use some help getting the boat out of the pond. We might need an extra-long rope to drag it to the edge where we can flip it over."

"What exactly did you put on your preferences in your BODS profile?" Brand asked, a look of puzzlement on his face.

"It doesn't matter what I put," Dillon said, taking a quick sip of the beer. "You'll have your chance to fill out your profile the way you like. I don't need to know what you put down."

"Emma said Leslie's working to restore an earlier version of the software," Brand continued. "What happened last night after we left her office? Did you break the system on purpose?"

"No, the lightning strike must have scrambled the system or hardware. I actually ran into Arianna coming out of the computer lab in the dark."

Emma's eyes widened. "You met last night?"

"We did, but it was in the dark because the electricity was off, and we made our way to the exit via the stairwell." All twenty flights. His lips twisted into a wry grin. "We never exchanged names."

Coop chuckled. "So, you didn't know who Ariana was until you met at the coffee shop?"

Dillon nodded. "That's right."

"And the sad fact is that BODS has a glitch. They probably weren't even supposed to be matched," Emma said. "Leslie is beside herself. She's still at the office with Tag trying to fix it."

"So, what's your plan for the evening, Romeo?" Ace asked Dillon. "Going to take your glitch date back to Austin? Or are you two staying for dinner?"

"Is there enough for us?" Dillon asked.

"You're going to keep her?" Brand asked. "After she nearly drowned you both?"

Dillon glared at his brother. "It was an accident. And yes, I'm going to keep her—continue our date through a meal, whether it's here or in Austin. Depending on how my brothers behave."

Brand held up his hands. "Just saying, BODS got it wrong. She doesn't fish, has never ridden a horse and probably likes cats more than dogs." He shook his head. "No use continuing down a dead-end path."

His hand tightening around the bottle of beer, Dillon's eyes narrowed. "She's not a dead end," he said. "She's pretty, really nice and means well. Which is more than I can say for you."

"I could say that about any golden retriever," Colton said and chugged the rest of his beer, setting the bottle on the rail beside him. "The question I have is, is she someone you can see yourself with for the long-term?"

"If you mean do I want to take her out again?" Dillon shrugged. "Maybe."

Colton whooped. "Hot damn, he's in love."

"That's ridiculous," Dillon said, though his pulse quickened, and his chest grew tight at the thought.

"I've only known her for less than twenty-four hours."

"You've heard of love at first sight," Ace said with a grin.

"We were in the dark at our first meeting," Dillon said. "I couldn't even see her. It doesn't count."

"I heard cheering," a voice said from the door. "Did I miss the excitement?" Ariana stepped out, wearing her long skirt, yellow, sleeveless sweater and boots. Her damp hair curled against her cheeks and across her shoulders, drying in the afternoon sun.

Dillon shook his head. "We were just celebrating the fact Colton had a thought. It's the first one he's had all year." He winked. "Can I get you something to drink?"

"What are you having?" she asked.

"Beer," he said. "I'm sure Emma has wine somewhere. Or if you don't like alcohol, we can offer you tea or a soda."

"I'll have a beer," she said.

Dillon turned to go back inside.

"I can get it," Ariana said. "I'm not good at fishing, but I can find my way around a kitchen. Just tell me where you keep the beer; I can get it myself."

"Stay," Emma said, waving a hand. "I'll get it. I need to grab the plates and silverware, anyway."

"I can help," Ariana offered.

"Thank you, but I have help." Emma smiled up at Coop as he followed her through the door.

The sound of his sister's giggle made Dillon smile. He was glad she'd found Coop. She'd spent far too long grieving for Marcus after his death. She deserved to be happy. Coop made her happy.

Though Emma had had to drag him into the matchmaking idea, Dillon truly hoped that he'd come out the other side as content as his sister.

His gaze went to Ariana. Could she be the one, despite BODS' malfunction? He hadn't thought the whole computer picking his match thing was legitimate to begin with. He'd rather take his chances and find a partner on his own. Since he'd already started work on his house, now might be a good time to look for a bride to help him fill it with love and the patter of little feet. Could Ariana be that bride he'd imagined himself with?

She wasn't tall and willowy like he'd imagined for himself, but he liked her dark red hair and her soft hazel eyes. And he liked the way her cheeks filled with color when she was embarrassed. Most of all, he liked how easily he could talk with her. He didn't feel like he had to be *on* all the time. She made him feel comfortable but, at the same time, physically excited by her nearness. When he'd kissed her, the dynamics of his feelings for her had changed entirely.

Now, he had a hard time thinking about anything else but kissing her again.

"Who's ready for a steak?" Ace asked. "The corn

and potatoes are done. I could use some help carrying the food inside to the dining room."

Ariana hurried down the porch steps and held out her hands.

Ace set a tray filled with foil covered cobs of corn in her hands. She smiled and turned toward the house.

Dillon took the tray of steaks and followed her inside. "First door on your right," he said.

Ariana entered the dining room and set the tray of corn in the middle of the table on a trivet.

The table has been set for seven people. Dillon pulled out the chair next to the seat he normally occupied. "You can sit beside me."

Ariana smiled about him. "Thanks."

Ace came in carrying a tray fill with baked potatoes wrapped in foil. He set it on the table and stood behind the seat at the head of the table while he waited for everyone else to enter the dining room.

Emma and Coop were the last to enter. They each carried glasses filled with ice water and set them beside the plates on the table.

Emma smiled. "Let's eat."

Dillon held the chair for Ariana. When she sat, he scooted the chair forward and took a seat beside her.

Emma took Coop's hand and looked around the table. "I know I don't do this very often, but would you mind if I said a prayer?"

Ace grinned. "Knock yourself out, Sis."

"Let's all join hands," she said, and waited a moment for everyone to join hands. "Dear Lord, thank you for this food we are about to eat. And Lord, we understand you have a plan for us. Please help us to accept your plan and go with it, whether it was what we anticipated or is something fresh and unexpected. Help us to make good choices and to be happy. Amen."

Everyone at the table echoed "amen" and released hands.

Dillon shot a glance at his sister. Was the prayer meant for him and Ariana? Was she telling them to ignore the fact that BODS had made a mistake? Did she want them to continue dating?

Emma smiled at Dillon. "You know we have a Hellfire firefighter picnic next Saturday at the county fairgrounds. You should bring Ariana."

"I don't know." The last thing Dillon wanted to do was hang around a bunch of people in the sunshine playing silly games, when he could be alone with Ariana somewhere more private. Even the pond sounded like a better idea.

"It's a lot of fun." Emma turned toward Ariana. "We play games, eat, mingle and get to know each other. And it's a fundraiser for the volunteer fire department in Hellfire. They do this once a year to raise money for the new equipment they desperately need."

"I need to look at my calendar," Ariana hedged.

"Me, too," Dillon said. "I have a project that's behind. I'm taking off this weekend, but I'm not sure I can take off next weekend, too."

"Well, you two think about it. It would be nice to support the firefighters. They're mostly volunteers, who give up their own time to help the community," Emma said.

"We'll be there," Colton said.

"Speak for yourself," Brand muttered.

"He'll be there," Ace said. "And so will I. The firefighters need the equipment. The least we can do is help them out."

The rest of the meal passed with Dillon's brothers picking at each other good-naturedly.

Dillon worried that they would scare off Ariana, but she laughed and joke with the best of them, even getting in a good jab or two that made his brothers smile.

When they were finished, Coop and Emma insisted on doing the dishes while the rest of them headed back to the porch.

Dillon leaned against a post while Ariana sat on the top step of the stairs.

I-lean, the black and white barn cat with three good legs and one missing a foot leaped up onto the porch, chased by Ruger, Ace's Australian Shepherd.

"Hey, boy," Ace squatted down and pulled the big dog into his arms, ruffling his fur. "Where have you been all day?"

"Terrorizing that poor cat, I'm sure," Colton said.

"You don't terrorize cats, do you, Ruger," Ace said, scratching the dog's belly.

With the dog otherwise occupied, the cat slowly limped across the porch, pausing only slightly at each man seated in rocking chairs or leaning against the rail. She didn't stop until she reached Ariana. I-Lean rubbed up against Ariana, purring like a motorboat engine.

Ariana held out her hand to the animal. "Hey, sweetie, is that big ol' dog getting all the attention?"

I-Lean rubbed her chin against Ariana's hand and let her scratch her behind the ears.

"I'll be damned," Brand said. "That cat doesn't like anybody."

"What's her name?" Ariana asked, looking up at Brand and Dillon.

"Her name is I-Lean, on account of the fact she has only three good feet," Ace said.

"Poor baby." Ariana frowned. "How did she lose the foot?"

"We don't know," Dillon said. "She appeared in the barn one day the way you see her now. She could have been born that way or lost it in a cat fight. We'll never know."

"You like cats?" Colton asked.

Dillon shot him a narrow-eyed glare. One he hoped Ariana wouldn't see.

"I do," Ariana said. "I always wanted one, but my

parents were allergic."

Brand sat in a rocking chair with his arms crossed over his chest. "What about dogs?"

Ariana smiled at Ruger. "I like them, too. Although, I've never owned one. The closest thing to a pet I ever owned was a goldfish I won at a county fair."

Colton raised an eyebrow toward Dillon.

Dillon's frown increased. If looks could kill, his brother would be dead.

"What do you think about the cliché that opposites attract?" Brand asked.

Dillon almost threw his hands in the air. Couldn't his brothers give it a rest?

"I think it makes sense," Ariana said. "I believe in balance. Nature has a way of correcting things that get out of balance. I think people need a person to balance them." She smiled. "My grandparents were a perfect example. He was a very grumpy man. She was a complete optimist. Her optimism balanced his grumpiness. My father was an introvert. My mother an extrovert. They balanced each other."

"Have you ever been around cattle?" Colton asked.

Dillon pushed away from the rail. "Look, Ariana isn't here to confront the inquisition. I only brought her out for a day on the ranch and to do a little fishing. That's it. She's not interviewing for the job of a ranch hand or anything else."

"They're not bothering me," Ariana said with a smile. "It's flattering that they're interested enough to ask me questions." She turned to Colton. "And no, I've never been around farm animals. I grew up in Austin, in an urban setting. But I love animals, and I like to learn about them."

"Now that you know all there is to know about Ariana, we'll be heading back to Austin," Dillon held out his hand to Ariana. "Ready?"

She laid her hand in his and let him draw her to her feet.

He circled his arm around her waist, wanting to protect her from his brothers' annoying questions.

Ace nodded toward the cat. "I think you've found a friend in I-Lean."

Ariana smiled. "She's beautiful. I hope Ruger doesn't hurt her."

"Don't worry about I-Lean. She's scrappy. She lets Ruger chase her," Ace said. "When she's had enough, she stands her ground, and he backs off."

"I'm glad she has that ability. When you're smaller, you learn to use your strengths to stand up for yourself." She looked Colton square in the eye. "I'm short, but, like I-Lean, I'm scrappy. I know you're only looking out for the best interests of your brother, so I don't take offense to your questions. You want to know more about me in case your brother and I decide to go out again."

She lifted her chin. "I'm five-feet-two-inches, my

hair really is red, it's not out of a bottle, and I like cats and dogs and children. I hope to have some of each someday. Until then, I'm happy teaching meditation techniques to stressed out corporate executives, stay-at-home housewives and soldiers with PTSD. I also teach yoga, which might not impress you, but it's another way I learned to get my balance back after the loss of my husband to cancer."

Ariana faced Ace. "Thank you for a lovely dinner and good company. If you have any more questions for me, Emma has my number. Give me a call. I'm an open book. I believe in being honest." She looked up at Dillon. "I'm ready."

Dillon grinned, hooked her arm and led her down the stairs. When he reached the bottom, he looked over his shoulder at his brothers, who were all watching Ariana as she walked toward his pickup. They didn't have to say anything. They had the look on their faces that said they'd been schooled, and they were impressed.

"Leaving already?" Emma asked as she came out onto the porch.

"Need to get Ariana back to her vehicle before they tow it out of the coffee house parking lot," Dillon said.

"That's a shame," Emma said. "If you stay just a few more minutes, you can watch the sunset. It's pretty amazing out here."

"I'll bring her out another time for the sunset,"

Dillon said.

"Thanks for cooking. Dinner was great," Ariana said.

"Thank you. We're glad you stayed." Emma smiled. "Will we see you back tonight, Dillon?"

He shook his head. "I'll stay in Austin tonight at the condo." Dillon opened the door for Ariana, gripped her around her waist and lifted her up into the cab.

She smiled down at him. "You make that look easy."

"It is."

"Well, thank you." She leaned down and pressed a kiss to his forehead, careful not to touch the bruise from the boat flipping. "I'm sorry I flipped the boat."

"I'm not. We got to spend a few short minutes alone together." He moved around the truck and climbed behind the steering wheel.

"But you nearly drowned," she said, continuing their conversation.

"It was worth it to me." He gave her a crooked grin. Once they passed through the ranch gate and turned onto the highway, he frowned. "No brothers around to annoy the hell out of us."

"Your brothers and sister care about you," she said softly. "You're lucky to have them."

He looked her direction again. "That's right, you didn't have any siblings."

"No. I always wanted brothers and sisters." She

stared out the window. "And when I do have children, I won't have just one. Children need siblings."

He nodded. "I have to agree. I can't imagine a life growing up without all of mine. We were never bored. Still, there are times I like my space."

She laughed. "I'll remember to flip a boat again when you want to be alone."

"With you," he added. "How about tomorrow?"

Her brow dipped. "What about tomorrow? You want me to flip a boat again?"

"No, but I figure we only have a day, maybe not even that long, until Leslie fixes BODS, and we have to meet our perfect match. How would you like to buck the system and go out with me again? I promise to take you to something more in line with what you like to do."

"I loved going fishing," she said. "I didn't even mind going swimming, once I knew you were okay."

"Yeah, but I want to do something you're familiar with, so you're not put into an uncomfortable position."

Her brow twisted. "I have a yoga class tomorrow in the morning, but the rest of the afternoon is free."

"Yoga?" He grimaced. "Do you have room for another student?"

She laughed. "I do, but are you sure you want to join the class? It's all older women. We take it really slow and easy."

"I get along really well with older women. My

mother was an older woman." His smile faded. "I don't have to wear yoga pants or a leotard, or anything like that, do I?"

"No. You can wear shorts and a T-shirt." She stared at him. "The ladies will be delighted. Be warned, though, they might get a little giddy around a good-looking man."

"I'll bring my back-off spray. What time?" he asked.

"It'll be early—nine in the morning. It gives them time to shower and change before church."

The drive back to Austin took only thirty minutes. The evening traffic had calmed, and they made it to the coffee house with no problems.

After Dillon helped Ariana down from her seat, he held on around her waist. "I'm glad my date turned out to be you," he said.

"After sitting in traffic, waiting for a wreck to clear, my stomach was knotted and I dreaded meeting a stranger," she said. "When you turned around, I felt better immediately." She leaned up on her toes and brushed her lips across his. "Thank you for being there."

He gathered her in his arms. "Thank you for being you. I feel like we bonded as friends in the dark." Then he crushed her mouth with his, deepening the little kiss she'd given him.

Ariana encircled the back of his neck with her hands and pressed her breasts to his chest.

He wanted so much more than just a kiss. When their lips finally parted, he leaned his forehead against hers. Was it too soon to ask her if she'd like to go back to his place and pick up where they'd left off?

"I'd better go," she said. "Thank you for today." She stepped back and smiled up at him. "See you tomorrow at nine?"

He nodded.

"If you change your mind, I'll understand," she said. "Not every man wants to be in a room full of older women. Especially doing yoga. I have other classes during the week where I have a good mix of men and women, if you'd rather come to one of those."

"I'll be there tomorrow at nine." He walked her to her car and opened her door for her after she unlocked it.

Before she got in, he kissed her again.

He could do that all night long and not get tired of it.

She looked up into his eyes and ran her tongue across her damp lips. "Goodnight, my stranger from the dark."

He chuckled. "Good night my redheaded stairwell girl."

He stepped back and watched as she backed out and drove away.

BODS couldn't have been wrong with this match. Dillon felt like they fit.

So what if she didn't fish or ride? So what if she liked cats better than dogs? When they kissed, none of that mattered.

Or had it been too long since he'd had a woman in his bed, and he was just a horny bastard?

No. If that had been the case, he would have asked her to go back to his condo. They would have made love, and he would never have arranged another date with her.

Instead, he'd let her go with a promise to be at a yoga class in the morning, the only man in a room with a dozen older women.

What had he been thinking?

Maybe it was his way of checking their compatibility by entering her world. He'd taken her into his, which had turned out fairly unfortunate. What could go wrong in a yoga class?

He'd spend an hour stretching muscles he never used. The ladies would get a good laugh at his form. Then he'd take Ariana out to a nice restaurant where they would sip wine and talk about...

Fishing?

Probably not.

The construction industry?

She wouldn't be interested.

Yoga?

Well, it would be a start. Maybe they had the same taste in music. They had to have something in common. BODS couldn't have been that messed up.

CHAPTER 9

ARIANA DRESSED for bed and had just laid down when she sat straight up again.

"Damn."

Dillon didn't know where her studio was.

Then she remembered she had his phone number because he'd texted her, and she'd responded. She reached for her phone on the table beside her. Looking for the text, she assigned his name and saved him as a contact.

Dillon Jacobs. She even liked the sound of his name. She closed her eyes and said it out loud, picturing the shadowy outline of the stranger in the BODS office before she'd seen his face. His voice had been what had drawn her to him. That deep, resonant tone that curled her toes.

Suddenly, she wanted to hear it again. She had the perfect excuse. He needed the address of her studio.

As she lay in her bed, with the lights off and nothing but the glow of her phone screen to illuminate the room, her hand hovered over his phone number.

"Oh, just do it," she murmured, and pressed the call button.

Her phone rang immediately. She realized her call was going out as another was coming in. The contact name on the incoming call read "Dillon Jacobs."

Her hand shook so hard she dropped her cellphone.

Ariana snatched up the phone and hit the button to receive the call. Smoothing her hair, she inhaled deeply and let the air out quickly. "Hello," she squeaked.

"Ariana?" That deep, sexy tone flowed through the phone and into every pore of her skin.

"Dillon," she said on a sigh and sank back on her pillow.

"I forgot to get the address of your studio."

"Oh," she said and sat up again. "Right. I was just about to call with that information." She gave him the address.

"Nine o'clock," he stated. "I'll be there."

Feeling like he was about to hang up, Ariana gripped the phone tighter. "Dillon?"

"Yes?"

"Uh...how's your head?" she asked.

"It's fine. I put an icepack on the lump, and it's gone down considerably."

"I'm glad." She lay back on the pillow again. "I guess you're going to sleep now?"

"I don't usually go to sleep this early," he said.

"Me either. I was thinking about reading a book or watching a show. I'm just not motivated to do either."

"I'm the same," he said. "I could go through the plans and emails related to the project I'm working, but when I gave the men the weekend off, I mentally checked out as well."

"What do you like to watch on television?" she asked.

"I'm pretty boring. I like watching anything to do with history or science. I'll watch some of the police procedural programs, too."

"I have a secret love of the British cooking shows," Ariana said.

"Do you like to cook?" he asked, his voice making her skin tingle with awareness.

"Sometimes. I'm not that good at making dinner, but I love to bake."

"What's your favorite, cakes or pies?"

"Pies. And fruit pies at that. None of those cream pies."

"That's too bad," he said.

"Why?" she asked, afraid she'd pointed out yet another difference between them and another reason BODS had gotten their match so completely wrong.

"That's bad because we'd have to fight over who got the last piece of apple pie."

She relaxed, a smile curling her lips. "I'd split it with you."

"Do you like any cakes?"

"I love brownies," she said. "Does that count in the cake category?"

"Absolutely." He paused then added. "Now, this is a deal-breaker question. Nuts or no nuts in your brownies?"

"Brownies aren't brownies without the nuts. And pecans over walnuts, all day long," she said.

"Good girl," he said. "We agree on more than one thing now. We'd better stop while we're ahead."

"Right. We should." She held the phone, not wanting to end the call. "Did you drive back out to the ranch?"

"No. I have a condo in Austin. I usually stay here during the week. The traffic getting in and out of the city can be difficult on good days, impossible on others."

"You're lucky. Not everyone can afford to have two places," she said.

"Having my own place allows me some peace and quiet away from my brothers. I look forward to having a place of my own someday on the ranch. I have the plans all drawn up and the site staked out. I just need to free up the crews to start construction. It'll have a huge porch wrapping around all sides with porch swings, rocking chairs, a couple of kids and dogs, someday."

"Sounds wonderful," Ariana said. "Which will come first, the kids or the dogs?"

"It will likely depend on the mother of my children. She might want to have a say in the matter."

A stab of longing tore at Ariana's heart. When BODS spit out the right match for Dillon, that lucky woman would be the one having Dillon's babies, not her. That made her sad.

"You still there?" he asked.

"I'm here," she whispered, her throat tightening. "Is it wrong of me to want Leslie to take a long time to fix BODS?"

Dillon chuckled. "No. I've almost called her twice today to ask her to stall. But that didn't seem fair to her other clients."

Ariana's heart warmed. Dillon had no desire to suffer through meeting a BODS's corrected match, any more than she did.

"So, after your yoga class, what do you usually do?" he asked, rustling sounding in the background as though he was getting more comfortable in his seat.

"I catch up on my grocery shopping and laundry. Nothing exciting."

"I could help you with the grocery shop," he said. "We could get the ingredients to make two apple pies."

Ariana laughed. "Two?"

"I'd want to make sure we had enough for both of us. Or, we could make one pie and a pan of nutty brownies."

"Shouldn't there be some protein and vegetables in there somewhere?" she asked.

"We could call out for pizza delivery."

"And that qualifies as protein and vegetables?" She laughed.

"If you get a pizza with everything on it, it will have protein and vegetables."

"You have a point."

"Of course, I do." He paused. "So, is there a pizza in our future together."

"And apple pie?" she asked.

"I like to think so."

"Makes perfect sense following a healthy dose of yoga in the morning," she said.

"Then it's a date," he said.

Ariana smiled into the phone. "It's a date."

"Who needs a computer system when you can find your own match in the dark."

"With your eyes closed," she said.

"You had your eyes closed?"

"I was trying to get my night vision faster after the lights went out," she said. "I thought it would improve if I closed my eyes, and then opened them."

A chuckle sounded in her ear. "Do you get the feeling we were meant to meet?"

She nodded, even though he couldn't see her. "It seems that way. Though, I don't think you were meant to get dumped into a pond trying to teach a neophyte how to fish."

His chuckle turned into a laugh. "I wish you could have seen yourself as you strung the worm on the hook."

"And I wish you could have seen yourself when the fish slapped you in the face." She laughed with him. "A very memorable day."

"Yes, it was," he said. "And not all bad. There were some highlights in there."

"Mine was when you turned around at the coffee shop," she said softly.

"That was one of mine. There were a couple others." His voice lowered, getting deeper and sexier.

"The kiss on the shore?" Ariana whispered.

"Definitely," he said. "And the one at the coffee shop not too long ago. I can still taste you on my lips."

Ariana touched her fingers to her lips where they still tingled from his touch.

"How many more hours until nine?" he asked.

"Too many," she responded.

"Tell me again about your techniques of meditation, because all I can think of is you. Especially when I close my eyes. I'm back in the BODS building in the dark, bumping into you, or walking down the stairwell for twenty flights."

Her heart swelled in her chest, and her pulse beat hard in her veins. "I could cancel my yoga class tomorrow."

"No," he said, his voice firm. "That's your business. I just want to get to know you better."

"Seems it might only show us how different we are."

"I don't think that's a bad thing," he said. "Didn't you say opposites attract for a reason?"

"Yes. But you also have to have things in common."

"We do," Dillon said.

"Apple pie!" they said at the same time.

A long, comfortable pause stretched between them

"Are you sleepy?" he asked

"A little," she admitted.

"Then I'll let you go to sleep. You need to be bright and cheerful for your class in the morning. Goodnight, Ariana."

"Goodnight, Dillon." She waited for a click or a dial tone indicating he'd ended the call. "Dillon?"

"Sorry. I thought you were going to end the call."

"I thought you were," she said with a smile on her lips. "Goodnight."

"Goodnight," he said. This time, he did end the call.

Ariana lowered the cellphone and stared at his name on the screen.

Dillon Jacobs.

Then she rolled onto her side, tucked her phone beneath her ear and closed her eyes, remembering the silhouette of his broad shoulders outlined in the faint glow of the distant exit sign. Something beautiful had happened that night the lights went out in a high-rise in Austin.

Ariana was determined to hold onto the memories as long as she could. Even if Leslie's computer system hadn't gotten it right.

Her last thought as she fell asleep was of the initials.

What did the B stand for in BODS?

Next meeting of the Good Grief Club, she'd ask Leslie.

DILLON LAY AWAKE WELL into the night, thinking about Ariana, the kiss and the conundrum of the BODS mistake in matching them.

They weren't alike in many ways. But he liked the way she made him feel calm and excited in the same breath. She wasn't anything like the women he'd dated in the past. But maybe that was a good thing. He'd never gone past a single date with most of them, finding himself bored after the first fifteen minutes.

Ariana wasn't experienced at anything to do with ranching. But that could be taught. Maybe. If not...so what? Why would she ever need to be a rancher?

Dillon and his brothers, along with Emma and Coop, could handle all the work on the ranch. If not, they could hire ranch hands. It wasn't like they couldn't afford it. Each of them had amassed their own fortunes either through day trading stocks or building their own businesses to the point they had accumulated significant wealth.

Why did his brothers think it was a requirement for any woman Dillon dated to be proficient at basic ranching tasks, like riding horses or mucking stalls?

Dillon's lips quirked.

Because they'd been pretty hard on Coop when he'd been matched with Emma. They'd put him through a pretty rigorous test of his worth on the ranch by inviting him to help them haul hay.

What they hadn't known was that Coop had spent summers between semesters at college hauling hay for pay. Not only did he know his way around a ranch, he loved horses and sports. He'd fit right in with the Jacobs brothers like one of their own.

At first, Emma had been irritated by how easily he'd assimilated into the family. She'd wanted to date and dump her match. Only, she'd ended up falling in love with the billionaire.

And they were perfect for each other. Unlike Dillon and Ariana, Emma and Coop had a lot in common. They knew ranching. Liked sports and could ride horses.

Did that mean any relationship Dillon and Ariana

would have could be doomed to failure from the start?

Dillon hoped not. He enjoyed talking with her. And helping her up into his truck. He liked how tiny her waist was and the sweet swell of her hips. He liked the fiery red of her hair and the lush hazel color of her eyes.

And he liked kissing her.

Colton had accused him of loving her.

No. That couldn't be. They hadn't known each other long enough.

Thus, the need to see her again. He knew there was something between them, but he wasn't exactly sure what it was or how long it would last. Only time would tell.

He set his watch to wake him up by five the next morning so that he could get up, go for a run to burn off energy, and then shower and be ready to meet her at her studio with a dozen other women.

He'd rather be alone with Ariana. At least in her class, he'd get to see her in her element and really get to know what she did best. She wouldn't have a following if she wasn't good at what she did.

Dillon fell asleep, only to be wakened what felt like a few minutes later when his alarm went off.

He rolled out of bed, slipped on his shorts and running shoes and went out into the early morning Austin downtown district. He jogged for three miles, moving through the streets dodging delivery vans and feeling the heartbeat of the beautiful city for what felt like the first time in a long time.

When he returned to his condo, he drank coffee and let his body cool before ducking into the shower. With thirty minutes to spare, he headed to the west side of Austin to Ariana's Zen studio.

Before he'd met Ariana, if anyone would've said he'd be going to a yoga class, he would've told them they were high on something. Yet, here he was pulling up to her studio along with the dozen women who paid her to lead the class. Hell, if he liked the effects of the exercises, he might just join them every Sunday. Sunday happened to be the only day he could reasonably attend on a regular basis.

He could imagine his brothers' reactions to his announcement that he'd be attending yoga classes on Sundays. Dillon didn't care. His brothers had to have something to pick on him about. But when shit hit the fan, they would always have his back—but not just his brothers. Emma was even more of a force to be reckoned with when someone threatened her family or friends.

Dillon held the door for all the gray-haired women, finally entering after the last one went inside. They all looked at him and smiled as they passed him going through the door.

One winked, said "Hubba Hubba" and pinched his chest. "Ooo...those are real," she murmured, and then walked away giggling.

He just smiled politely at the woman and refrained from engaging. He wasn't there for them. Dillon had come to see...

Ariana stood in front of the class, dressed in a black form-fitting tank top and yoga pants. Her feet were bare, and her hair was pulled up into a ponytail, high on the crown of her head.

She smiled at him then turned her attention to the ladies in the class.

Dillon took a mat from the stack in the corner, like the ladies did, but chose to position his at the very back of the room.

For the next hour, Ariana led them from one pose to another, holding the poses for what felt like an excruciating time before releasing them.

The older women in front of him tried on occasion to help him get the poses right, but he shook his head, pressed his finger to his lips and pointed to the instructor.

The ladies nodded and went back to posing, which they did much better than Dillon. He told himself they'd had many years of practice. That this was his first time, and he wasn't sure if he'd do it again. By the time they finished up, he was certain he'd pulled a muscle in his calf and another in his gluteus maximus...hell...in his ass. He carried his mat to the corner, limping slightly.

"Congratulations," a voice said from behind him. "You made it through your first yoga class."

He turned to find Ariana standing behind him, looking like she hadn't broken a sweat, whereas he needed another shower. "Thanks. I have a new appreciation for the art." He rubbed his hand over his right butt cheek.

"It looks easy, just a bunch of poses, but when you hold them for so long, it exerts pressure on the muscles, strengthens them and helps tremendously with balance. It also improves flexibility and helps to prevent back pain. As well, yoga inspires mental calmness."

"I feel calm already."

When the last client exited the studio, leaving the two of them alone, Dillon pulled Ariana into his arms and tipped up her chin. "I haven't stopped thinking about this since I left you at the coffee shop yesterday." He captured her lips in a gentle kiss that grew more insistent.

She wrapped her arms around his waist, pressed her hips to his, her breasts to his chest and melted against him with a smothered sigh.

They stood locked in each other's embrace until the need to breathe forced them to lift their heads.

Dillon stared down into Ariana's eyes. "I could do this all day, but we have shopping to do."

She nodded. "I'd suggest we stay here and continue what we were doing, but I don't have food or a kitchen here." She cupped his cheek. "I thought we could buy the ingredients to make apple pie and pizzas rather than ordering out."

"Your place or mine?" he asked. "I have a gourmet kitchen I never use."

"Yours, but we can stop by mine. I have a pizza stone and pie plates." She tilted her head. "Do you have either of those?"

He shook his head. "I think I have a grill and a fry pan."

"In a gourmet kitchen..." She shook her head. "Why do you have a chef's kitchen if you're not using it?"

"I bought the place from a chef who moved to New York City. I liked the location and the view. The kitchen was a bonus. Well, if I would actually use it."

She brushed her lips across his briefly. "Come on. I can't wait to see this kitchen."

And he couldn't wait to have her in his condo. He wasn't sure what would happen there, but he hoped she'd stay for more than pizza and apple pie.

CHAPTER 10

ARIANA AND DILLON spent the next hour shopping for the groceries they'd need for the pizzas and pies. Then they swung by her place for mixing bowls, pie plates, the pizza stone and utensils they'd need to make it all happen.

When they arrived at Dillon's condo building, Ariana stared up at the high rise. "This is a building of condos?"

"No, it's an office building. I own the only condo located in the penthouse suite at the top." He pointed to the very top of the building, where glass windows reflected the sunlight and clouds.

"How much of the top floor do you own?" she asked.

His mouth twisted. "All of it."

She blinked, her heartbeat fluttering in her chest. "Your condo is the entire top floor?"

He nodded, hooked her arm and led her into the building, past a guard at the front desk and to an elevator that required a special key card to allow them access to the penthouse.

Ariana had been to some nice places in her life, but she'd never been in a penthouse like the one she stepped into from the elevator.

The foyer floor was covered in shiny white marble tiles that lead into a living area with floor-to-ceiling windows. The room itself was stunning with white leather furniture, dark accent tables and immaculate artwork adorning what walls there were.

But it was the view that commanded her attention. She walked straight across the floor to the windows and stared out at the city of Austin spread out before her. "Wow."

Dillon came up behind her. "That's how I felt when I walked into the suite. Nothing else seemed to matter."

"I see why you like it," she said, her voice quiet, feeling awestruck. "It's stunning."

"It's even more impressive at night."

"I can imagine."

"Wait and see." He carried the bags of groceries through the living area to a massive kitchen with a six-burner gas stove, double ovens and a commercial-sized refrigerator.

"You weren't kidding when you said it was a

gourmet kitchen," Ariana said. "Was it all like this when you bought it?"

"No, I gutted most of it, except the kitchen. The chef who owned it spent all his money there. The rest of the place needed updating and upgrading."

"You did an amazing job," she said. "And what a difference from your home on the ranch."

"I make my living constructing and renovating beautiful buildings."

She smiled. "You did tell me you were in construction. Business must be good."

He unloaded the contents of a grocery bag. "It is. Now, are we making pizza? Or what?"

They spent the next hour and a half rolling out dough and cutting up vegetables and fruit for pizza and apple pie.

At one point, they got into a flour fight, dusting each other with a fine layer of white powder.

Ariana couldn't remember when she'd laughed so hard. Or kissed so deeply. Every step of the way, they touched, nibbled on each other and tasted. Cooking with Dillon was a kind of sensual dance. Foreplay.

By the time the pizza was cooked, she wasn't hungry for food. She was hungry for him.

Ariana set the pizza on the white quartz countertop to cool then ran the pizza cutter over it, making eight equal slices. She checked the status of the pie she'd just put in the oven and looked over at Dillon.

His gaze captured hers. "Hungry?" he asked, his voice more of a low growl.

"Yes," she said, her eyes narrowing a she stalked toward him.

"Want some pizza?"

"No." She took his hand in hers. "We have an hour of baking time before the apple pie is finished."

His brow wrinkled. "You want to wait for the apple pie to be done before eating dinner?"

She shook her head. "No, I want you to show me the rest of your place."

He slipped his arm around her and pulled her up against him to nuzzle her neck. "Did I tell you there's a hot tub in the master bedroom?"

"No, you didn't." She looked up into his face as she reached for the hem of her tank top and pulled it up over her head. "Show me."

"It would be my pleasure." He scooped her up in his arms and carried her through the living room to a set of double doors that opened into the master suite.

A king-sized bed was centered against one wall and there was a sitting area with a couch, a chaise lounge and a gas fireplace in the corner. Again, windows stretched floor-to-ceiling with another glorious view of the city below. On the other side of the room was another set of double doors leading into a bathroom that was bigger than Ariana's house. On one side was a sunken hot tub surrounded by white marble tile and more windows.

Dillon set Ariana on her feet and turned on the jets in the hot tub.

Ariana reached for the hem of his shirt and dragged it up as high as she could reach. He took over from there and pulled it over his head, tossing it to the floor. Then he hooked his thumbs in the elastic waistband of her yoga pants and panties and slid them down her hips and thighs, dropping down on one knee to take them to her ankles.

She shivered as cool air hit her naked skin. Her nipples puckered, not from the chill in the air, but in anticipation of what would come next.

Dillon stood, his hands trailing up her calves and thighs as he came to his feet.

Ariana slid her hands into the waistband of his shorts, pushed them over his hips and down his legs. His cock sprang free, hard and straight as she dropped the shorts to the floor, and he stepped out of them.

They stood before each other, completely naked.

"You are a beautiful woman, Ariana," he said.

"You're a beautiful man, Dillon."

"What are we waiting for?" With a grin, he lifted her up and deposited her into the hot tub.

The heated water enveloped Ariana as she sank down until she was in up to her shoulders.

Dillon reached into a nearby drawer and extracted an accordion of foil packets, dropping them on the surface surrounding the hot tub. He joined her in the water and pulled her into his arms.

"I've never done it in a hot tub," she admitted.

"We don't have to do anything but enjoy the water," he said.

She laid her hands on his shoulders and straddled his lap. "It's been a long time for me."

"We'll take it slowly," he said. "If this is what you want."

"I want," she said and reached for one of the little packets. She tore it open and stared down at the bubbling water. "Please don't let me make a disaster of this like I did with the fishing."

"Let me." He smiled, kissed her lightly, took the condom from her and rolled it over his engorged shaft.

She let go of the breath she'd been holding and lowered herself over him until his sheathed cock nudged her entrance.

His brow dipped. "Don't you want to take it slow? Maybe indulge in a little foreplay?"

"Cooking with you was all the foreplay I could stand and not take you inside me. Please," she whispered.

His hands resting on her hips pushed downward as he thrust upward, sliding into her.

She drew in a ragged breath, liking the way he filled her and made her feel a part of him. She pressed her heels against the bottom of the tub and rose up, letting him slide back out of her all the way to the tip of his shaft. Then she sank down again with the pressure of his hands bringing her back to him.

Dillon took control, guiding her up and down as he thrust in and out of her. As the pace increased, the jets pummeled their bodies and the water splashed over the rim.

Ariana rode Dillon, her body tensing as she climbed that slope to the very top.

When he thrust once more and buried himself deep inside her, she shot over the edge, her channel throbbing around him, the tingling electrical sensations rippling from her core outward to the very tips of her fingers and toes. "Oh, Dillon. Sweet Jesus, yes!"

He laughed and plunged once more into her, holding her down on him until he'd spent himself, his cock jerking with each spasm.

When they both came back to earth, they sank deeper into the tub and touched each other all over, exploring the other's body until their skin shriveled and the alarm on the stove in the kitchen alerted them to check the pie in the oven.

"I'll get it," Ariana said, climbing out of the tub.

"I'll help." Dillon got out behind her, snagged a towel from a rack and wrapped it around her. He grabbed one for himself, hitched it around his hips and hurried after her to the kitchen.

Ariana pulled the apple pie from the oven and set it on the stovetop to cool.

"Are you ready to eat?" she asked. "The pizza is cold."

"Mmm. I don't give a damn about the pizza." He turned her around to face him, and then lifted her up to sit her on the counter. "I didn't get to taste the appetizer." He parted her legs, slipped the towel from around her body and stepped between her knees.

"You left the protection in the bathroom," she reminded him.

He shook his head. "Won't need it for what I have in mind." He captured her mouth with his and kissed her long and hard, sliding his tongue over hers. Leaving her lips, he trailed his mouth over her jaw and down the long line of her throat to where the pulse beat fast at the base. He didn't linger there but moved lower to capture a nipple between his teeth, rolling it until it hardened into a tight little bead.

Ariana's back arched, pressing her breast deeper into his mouth.

He sucked it in, pulling hard.

She gasped and clung to him as he flicked the tip and nibbled. Then he moved to the other breast, applying the same technique there before he left to explore her torso, traveling across each rib and lower still to the hair covering her sex.

He dropped to a knee and parted her folds with this thumbs.

Ariana's breath caught and held in her throat as he flicked her clit with the tip of his tongue.

A rush of air left her lungs, and she threaded her fingers through his hair, dragging him closer.

He flicked that highly sensitive nubbin of flesh again setting off an eruption of sensations so powerful they made Ariana shake with the intensity.

Dillon increased his offensive, taking her with his mouth, conquering her with an orgasm that shook her to her very center.

She leaned back on her hands, her head thrown back, her body quivering with her release.

When she came back to her senses, Dillon stood there, a smile on his face and a slice of pizza in his hand. "Hungry?"

"Starving," she said and took the slice from him. A sun-dried tomato slipped out of the cheese and fell onto her left breast. When she started to scoop it off with her finger, he grabbed her wrist.

"That's mine," he growled and bent to suck it off, licking the tomato sauce from her skin. "Now, if anyone asks me what you taste like, I can honestly say pizza." He grinned and turned her hand to take a bite of her pizza.

For the rest of the afternoon, they ate, slipped back into the hot tub, showered, napped in the king-sized bed and explored every inch of each other's bodies.

When night fell, they cocooned themselves in a sheet and sat on the floor by the window, staring out at the blanket of lights below that made up the city of Austin.

Ariana sighed, leaning into his naked body. "You must love it here."

"It was just another place to sleep, until someone covered me in flour, showed me how to make pizza on a stone and added raisins to my apple pie. Who would have thought those things would make this mausoleum of a condo come alive?"

"You really do love the ranch, don't you?" she said, snuggling into the crook of his arm.

"It's my home. I feel more myself there. Making the money I do, I can afford all this, and it's convenient when I'm working in town, but my heart belongs on the ranch. I'm really just a country boy who likes getting his fingers dirty."

"I like that about you. I would never have guessed you lived in a place like this. It's beautiful, and I see why you love it," she waved toward the view, "but it's not you."

He leaned his cheek against the top of her head. "I'm working on it. I have a house plan designed. I just needed the motivation to start the work."

"And you have it now?"

He nodded. "I have site managers on all my projects. I need to trust them to do their jobs, so I don't have to be so hands-on."

She nodded. "And then you'll be less stressed and able to enjoy what you've accomplished." Ariana turned and brushed her lips across his. "I should be going back to my place."

"You could stay here," he suggested.

As much as she wanted to... "It's too soon. I've loved spending the day with you, but you have your project to check on in the morning, and I have to open my studio bright and early." The thought of leaving made her wish she could cancel classes for the next day and stay with Dillon. But then, he had a job as well. They both needed to focus on life outside the amazing bedroom with the hot tub they'd made love in twice.

Dressing became a game of on and off, tickling and kissing until they fell into the bed naked and made love one last time.

Exhausted, and knowing the morning would feel like it came too soon, Ariana finally managed to get all her clothes on and helped Dillon button his shirt. "I had an amazing weekend."

"Me, too," he said looping his arm around her waist as they headed for the elevator.

The trip back to her house didn't take nearly long enough. Ariana hated having to say goodbye. The weekend had been magical. She had no idea whether or not he would call her again. If he didn't, she'd be incredibly sad. But they'd gone into the weekend with no expectations of a future relationship. That didn't stop her from wanting one.

Dillon got out of his truck and came around the

front hood to open her door. When she turned to climb down, he gripped her around the waist and helped her to the ground, his hands still holding onto her.

She couldn't stop herself from asking. "Will I see you soon?"

Dillon stared down into her eyes. "I have to work late hours this week in order to get my project back on track. Can I call you?"

She smiled and nodded. "I understand."

Dillon was a busy man. He didn't make the kind of money he made without sacrificing his time.

Ariana refused to be one of those women who demanded he call and spend every evening with her. If he wanted to, he'd call. If he wanted her, he'd make the effort to see her when he could.

"Goodnight, Dillon," she said and rose up on her toes to press a kiss to his lips. When she started down to stand flat on her feet, she was stopped by the arm encircling her middle tightening. Her lips curled in a smile. He still wanted her.

"You call that a kiss?" he asked, raising an eyebrow.

"It was a start," she said. "If a man's interested, he'll take it home."

"Oh, I'm interested." He crushed her to him and plundered her mouth.

When he finally broke for a breath, he stared down into her eyes. "Thank you."

He took her keys from her fingers, inserted one into the lock, twisted and then pushed open the door.

"I'd invite you in," she said, "but you need the rest."

"As do you." He stepped back. "Close and lock the door. I won't leave until I know you're safely inside."

After another soul-defining kiss Ariana slipped through her door, closed and locked it. Then she leaned against the panel and slowly slid to the ground. What the hell had just happened?

Marrying her high school sweetheart hadn't prepared her for spending a weekend making love with the hottest cowboy in Texas.

The sound of his truck starting and pulling out of her driveway made her want to run out and beg him not to go.

She clenched her fists and fought that urge, telling herself, she couldn't show him just how much the time she'd spent with him meant to her. Based on his penthouse, he was very wealthy. He probably had women throwing themselves at him every day of the week.

She wasn't a gold digger. In fact, his wealth intimidated the hell out of her. She needed time away from him to think about what was best for her and for him.

If she continued to see him, would she be the right person for him? BODS had been broken when the system matched them. What if the right woman was out there, and Ariana stood in the way of Dillon meeting her?

To be fair, what if the right man for her was out there, waiting to be matched to her by Leslie's system?

Ariana leaned her head back against the panel and groaned. She didn't have the energy or heart capacity to fall in and out of love. Losing her husband had taken a huge toll on her. She couldn't lose again. She might be better off ending whatever it was she had between her and Dillon before it got any deeper.

Pushing to her feet, she trudged through her bedroom to the bathroom where she stripped out of her clothes and ducked into the shower, hoping the water would wash away her worries. After several minutes beneath the spray, she had to give up. The shower only reminded her of spending time bathing with Dillon, making love in the hot tub.

After drying off, she slipped into a T-shirt and panties, turned the air conditioner down to a cool sixty-eight and climbed between the sheets. Her cellphone lay charging on the nightstand beside her.

She looked over at it, tempted to text Dillon. He wasn't coming to her yoga class in the morning and, if he did, he already knew how to get there. She hadn't forgotten anything at his condo, and they hadn't made plans to meet again the next day or the day after. Hell, they hadn't agreed to anything for the entire week.

Was this Dillon's way of letting her down easy? Drop her off and fade away?

She lay down on the pillow, staring up at the ceiling. This was hard. She'd never dated someone like Dillon. She'd never dated anyone but Sam. She rolled onto her side and punched her pillow.

Go to sleep. Forget about him. You'll never hear from him again.

Her cellphone chirped and vibrated on her nightstand.

Ariana flipped over, grabbed the device and stared at the screen.

Dillon Jacobs.

Sweet Jesus, it was him. And he wasn't texting, he was calling.

She hit the talk button and answered. "Did you get lost?" Ariana forced a laugh, her voice sounding breathless, not at all normal.

"Did I catch you at a bad time?"

Oh, hell no. Anytime you catch me is the right time. "I just got out of the shower and was crawling into bed. You make it back to your place?"

"If I said I was still parked in your driveway, would you let me in?"

Ariana sat up straight in bed. "Are you?"

He chuckled, making that low, deep, sexy sound that made her knees go weak. "Sadly, no. I made it back to my condo and realized I left something at your house."

Ariana frown. "You did? You didn't even come in."

"No, I didn't. But you did. I left you at your house. This condo feels so much bigger and empty without you in it, making pizza and apple pie."

She laid back on her pillow, a smile curling her lips. "It is a big place."

"Too big for just me."

"You did an amazing job on the renovations," she said. "It's beautiful."

"You're beautiful."

"You're not so bad yourself," she said. "Is that all you called about?"

"Yeah," he said, "No. When will I see you again?"

Relief rushed through her. Forcing humor into her tone, she said, "You're the one with a project to catch up on."

He sighed. "I have a feeling I'll be working late every night this week, which means I won't see you. Will you be awake after ten?"

"I usually don't go to sleep until after eleven."

"Can I call you then?"

She smiled, cradling the phone in her hand, wishing it was Dillon's cheek. "Yes. I'd like that."

"Then it's a phone date," he said. "Tomorrow at ten."

"Tomorrow at ten," she confirmed. "Goodnight, Dillon."

"Ariana?" Dillon called out.

"Yes?"

"One other question." He paused. "And I don't want you to think less of me for asking."

"I won't," she said. "Go ahead and ask."

"What do you sleep in?"

Her core heated, and her temperature rose. "Why do you ask?"

"I'm lying here naked, wishing you were lying beside me. It helps to know what you're wearing."

A shiver of desire rippled through her. She hit the speaker button on the phone dropped it on the comforter. Then she sat up, ripped her T-shirt over her head, yanked her panties down her legs and flung them across the room. "I'll tell you what I'm wearing," she said, dropping her voice to what she hoped was a smooth, sexy tone. "Not a damned thing."

CHAPTER 11

DILLON SPENT the days of that week working to get the project back on track. They were so close to finishing that he refused to be derailed. Where he could, he helped out, calling for backup crews to complete some of the trim work, a plumber to help their fulltime plumber catch up, and another cleaning crew to start removing the excess material they wouldn't need to finish the work. He was with his site foreman most of the day and well into the evening, with men working both an early shift and a late shift to compress the schedule.

Every night at ten, when he would collapse exhausted in his bed, he wouldn't go to sleep until he called Ariana.

She'd be there to talk to him, her voice so beautiful and calming. He'd tell her about his day, and she'd fill him in on some antics of a yoga group or one of her meditation sessions. She told him she'd invested in a fishing pole and was practicing her casting in her backyard. So far, she'd snagged a tree, the gutter and her own hair. But she was making progress.

"I'm going to give you this fishing pole to replace the one I'm sure is at the bottom of the pond with your tackle box," she'd said.

He'd told her that wasn't necessary, but she'd insisted. He'd also told her that his brothers had retrieved the boat the day after it capsized and it was fine, sitting on the bank of the pond, waiting for her next fishing lesson.

Ariana had laughed, the sound so soft and happy, Dillon smiled. "I will get you back out there, and we will catch a fish."

"From the shore. I'm convinced I can't fish and boat at the same time," she said. "I'm one of those who can't walk and chew gun at the same time. I'd trip or choke on my gum."

The week flew by. Dillon worked hard to get things squared away at work so that his crew and he could have the weekend off again. He wanted to take Ariana to the Hellfire firefighter fundraiser on Saturday. He hadn't said anything yet, in case things didn't work out and he had to work the weekend. The crew had worked late every night, seeming to focus better when he was on site. When Friday rolled around, Dillon met with his site foreman and told him the crew wouldn't have to work the weekend.

A cheer went up when the foreman passed on the news to the crew.

Dillon had pulled out his cellphone with the intention of calling Ariana, when an incoming call made his phone chirp. He glanced at the name on the screen and grinned. "Hey, little sis. What's up?"

"Dillon. We haven't seen you at home lately."

"This project has me working too late to make it out to the ranch."

"We figured that much," she said. "I wanted to let you know that Leslie finally got BODS up and running with the backup copy. She ended up having to install a new server and reload all the data that was stored in the cloud."

"That's good," Dillon said, a flicker of unease forming in his belly.

"I thought it would be a good idea for you to give it another try. Maybe even bring your new match to the firefighter fundraiser tomorrow."

"No," he said, his tone flat and final.

She laughed. "Aren't you even curious who BODS will match you with?"

"No," he repeated. He didn't want to meet anyone else.

"Leslie and I are meeting with the Good Grief

Club today. Ariana's supposed to be there. Leslie is going to see if Ariana is ready to meet her true match."

Dillon's hand tightened on his cellphone. He didn't know what to say. He sure as hell didn't want Ariana to give BODS another chance. He liked her. A lot. If she went out with her BODS match, she might find someone more suited for her than him. Which would be good for her, but what about him?

"You know it wouldn't hurt to give it a second chance," Emma said. "Leslie feels really bad about the glitch and wants to make it up to you and Ariana."

"What if we don't want a second chance?" he asked.

"Are you answering for Ariana? What if that second chance guy truly is her perfect match? You like her, don't you?"

"Yes." More than he was ready to admit to his sister.

"If you like her that much, don't you want her to be happy?"

"Yes, of course I do." He didn't like the direction Emma was taking with this conversation. He was thinking the same thing, only he wasn't ready to admit it and concede.

"If BODS finds her perfect match, she has a chance at true happiness. After losing her husband to cancer, she deserves to be happy again, doesn't she?"

Damn Emma. Damn her to hell. Dillon ran a hand through his hair, wishing he hadn't answered his sister's call. He would've already asked Ariana to the firefighter fundraiser, and this wouldn't even be an issue.

His conversations with Ariana each night had meant the world to him. She…balanced him. Made him feel calm and happy for the first time since he'd started his own construction company. If the real BODS match was what would make her the happiest, he couldn't be the one to keep that from happening. Oh, but he wanted to. He wanted her for himself.

He sighed into the phone. "If Ariana wants to give BODS a second chance, I won't stand in her way."

"And if she goes for the second chance, will you?" Emma pushed.

If Ariana chose to go for the BODS true match and found him to be the one for her, Dillon wouldn't care if he fell off the face of the earth. "I don't care."

"I'll let you know what happens. You won't regret it. BODS really does work," Emma said. "Later."

Dillon ended the call and stared at his cellphone. He'd been ready to call Ariana and ask her to the fundraiser. His heart had been beating fast in anticipation of hearing her voice when she said yes.

He slipped his phone into his pocket and threw himself into work. He picked up a shovel and removed debris from the site. They had crews for that kind of work, but he needed manual labor that worked him hard and made him forget.

Only, with every shovelful of construction debris he threw into the wheelbarrow, he cursed himself for agreeing to step out of Ariana's way.

They were so new to their connection, Dillon didn't feel he had a handle on just what their relationship was. He didn't feel like he had any right to tell her who she could and couldn't go out with. He hoped she'd only want to go out with him, but that had to be her call.

For the rest of the day, he stewed on what Ariana's response might be to Leslie's offer to produce her true BODS match.

ARIANA SAT in the conference room in the BODS offices where the Good Grief Club had chosen to meet that month. Leslie and Emma, sat across from her, Ava and Fiona. They'd brought their own drinks and lunches, and Leslie had provided a tray of cookies for dessert.

Ariana couldn't help but smile as she sat in the BODS office. The last time she'd been there, had been her first meeting with Dillon, the tall, dark stranger who'd walked with her down twenty flights of stairs when the lights and elevator had been on the blitz.

"You'll be happy to know that Tag and I finally got BODS up and running. We installed a backup from a couple days before the storm, and a new server and modem since both took a hit by the lightning, and now everything appears to be up and running correctly."

Fiona, Ava and Emma all clapped, shaking Ariana out of her happy reminiscing. "What? Oh, that's really good news." She gave Leslie half a smile.

"Speaking of working correctly," Leslie segued into her next topic, "I'd like to run your match."

Ariana shook her head. "That won't be necessary."

"But I feel so awful," Leslie said. "I promised you a perfect match. When the system malfunctioned, I worried that you and Dillon would lose confidence in BODS. I was glad I caught you both with the news before you went out." She frowned. "You did cancel the date, didn't you?"

Ariana couldn't lie, so she shrugged instead. "I went fishing."

"With Dillon," Emma said with a grin. "It was an unqualified disaster."

"I'm sorry to hear that," Leslie said. "But then Dillon wasn't meant to be your match. I'm sure BODS will find the right one for you."

"I'm not interested in finding the right match," Ariana said. "I...I don't think I'm ready, after all."

"Of course, you are," Ava said. "You need to get

out there. You're young and beautiful. And, if you want children, you really can't wait much longer."

"I'm happy the way I am," Ariana said. They didn't have to know that she and Dillon were talking every night. Leslie might take issue with the two of them still "seeing" each other after she'd told them BODS had malfunctioned.

"Please," Leslie said. "If you don't give it a second chance, you might go through your life wondering if your perfect match is still out there."

"I can live with that."

Emma reached out and patted her hand. "If it makes it any easier, Dillon said he wouldn't stand in your way if you decided to give BODS another shot at finding your match."

Ariana's heart sank to the pit of her belly. "Dillon said that?"

Ava's eyebrows shot up. "Am I missing something?" She looked from Ariana to Emma and back. "Did you go out with Dillon even after Leslie said BODS screwed up?"

Ariana's cheeks heated. "I was already on the way to meet him and late. It didn't seem right to cancel at the last minute." She shrugged. "He got the same call and felt the same way, so we agreed to go out on a friendly basis." She smiled. "He took me fishing."

"Something he loves to do, that Ariana had never done," Emma said with a grin. "Tell them what happened."

Her cheeks on fire now, Ariana ducked her head. "I flipped the boat...with us in it."

"The point is," Emma continued, "Dillon was looking for someone who likes the outdoors, who would fish and ride horses with him. Ariana has never been fishing or riding horses."

"She could learn," Ava countered.

Emma continued. "Ariana was looking for someone low-key. Dillon is anything but low-key. Their profiles couldn't possibly have matched."

"That was caused by the glitch," Leslie said, shaking her head. "The thunderstorm jacked up the software and hardware. It took all week to fix. But now it's ready to go." She smiled. "I can have your match for you in just a few minutes."

"Dillon said he wouldn't stand in your way," Emma reminded her. "What do you have to lose?"

Her heart. Ariana lifted her chin. "Whatever."

"So, it's a go?" Leslie asked, her face brightening with a smile.

"I guess." Ariana looked down at her cellphone, her link to Dillon while he'd been working long hours all week. They'd spend two hours each night talking about the news, travel and sometimes, nothing at all, just talking. Had that meant nothing to him?

"I'll be right back," Leslie said.

Emma hopped up. "I'll just go with her." She grinned. "I'm so excited for you."

"If you'll excuse me, I need to call my sitter." Ava pushed back her chair and left the conference room.

Fiona turned to Ariana. "I get the feeling you don't want to go through with this second chance."

Ariana sighed, her gaze still on the phone. "I'm not so sure BODS really works."

"It worked for me, Emma, and for Leslie and Ava. There's no reason it won't work for you." Fiona reached out and took Ariana's hand. "What's really eating at you?"

A tear slipped for Ariana's eyes and dropped onto Fiona's hand. She wiped away others she couldn't keep from falling. "We weren't supposed to be matched."

"You and Dillon?" Fiona asked.

"Yes."

"You're falling for him, aren't you?" Fiona pulled her rolling chair closer and put her arm around her. "Sweetie, sometimes love hurts. You know that."

"I didn't think I could love anyone but Sam," Ariana sniffed. "We were so much alike in every way. We never really dated anyone else. It was so easy to marry him and hard to lose him."

"And Dillon isn't anything like Sam," Fiona stated.

"Nothing at all like Sam." Ariana looked up into Fiona's eyes. "But he's so animated, full of life and interesting. And we love to cook together. He wants to teach me how to fish and ride. And I want to learn."

"So, what's keeping you two from doing all that?" Fiona asked.

"BODS."

"What?" Fiona's brow creased.

"Our match was a mistake. Our preferences don't match. We're so different."

"When I took your meditation class, you talked about balance. For every action there's a reaction. For things that are off balance, nature has a way of providing the balance. You were never off balance with Sam. You two were perfectly in balance."

"Exactly. Which makes me and Dillon so wrong for each other."

"Wrong," Fiona said. "He leans one way, you lean the other, and in so doing, you create a perfect balance."

Ariana laughed through her tears. "If only I'd applied that principle when we were on the boat."

Fiona smiled. "Tell Leslie you're not interested in another match. You and Dillon are perfect together."

"I can't," Ariana said. "Dillon said he wouldn't stand in my way. That means he's not as committed to us as I am."

"You're putting words in that man's mouth. That can never be a good thing. Why don't you call and talk to him about it? There might be a perfectly good reason he said that to his sister."

"I don't want him to think I'm desperately

clinging to him—God, though I want to. He could have anyone. Why would he want me?"

"Because you're beautiful and kind," Fiona said. "Any man would be lucky to have your heart. Don't sell yourself short."

"It's hard not to. The man is loaded. Did you know that?" Ariana looked into her eyes. "He owns an entire top floor of an office building—and it's just his in-town home."

Fiona smiled. "That's why it's called BODS."

Ariana's brow dipped. "I don't understand. I never could figure out what the B stood for."

Fiona's smile broadened. "Billionaire. As in Billionaire Online Dating Service. It's an elite service just for people like Dillon, Coop and Gage, who have money, but don't have the time or patience to weed through all the gold diggers to find a gem of a woman who will love them for themselves."

Ariana sat back in her seat, her head spinning. "You're kidding me."

"No, ma'am," Fiona patted her hand. "Leslie vets everyone she invites to enter their profiles into the BODS database. She trusts you and knows you would only date or marry someone for love, not money."

"Frankly, the money thing intimidates the hell out of me," Ariana admitted. "Maybe it's right of Leslie to find me another match. I'd never want Dillon to think I love his money more than him."

"You do love him, don't you?" Fiona gave her a

crooked grin. "And you're thinking it's too soon. For me...when I knew...I knew. Time only validated my suspicions."

Ariana chewed on her bottom lip as she pondered her dilemma. "Still, if he wants me to give the BODS system another chance, so be it. He doesn't care enough to fight for me. My feelings for him must be one-sided."

"Seriously, you should talk to him. Sometimes, talking clears things up before they get blown out of proportion."

"If he calls me tonight, I will," Ariana promised. How she'd bring it up, she wasn't quite sure, but she'd do it.

Emma poked her head into the conference room. "Fiona, could you help me for a moment. I need for you to reach something for me."

Fiona glanced once more at Ariana. "Don't give up, yet." She looked up at Emma. "Coming."

Ariana sat in the room by herself, pondering Fiona's words. Should she fight for Dillon? Did he want her to? Was he bored and tired of their nightly chats?

She thought back. Dillon had initiated all of the phone calls. If he was tired of her, wouldn't he just stop calling?

Her head hurt from all the second-guessing. She buried her face in her hands and applied pressure to the bridge of her nose. Why did falling in love have to be so damned hard?

The door opened and Ava returned, followed by Fiona, Emma and, finally, Leslie.

Leslie had a file folder in her hand. She set it on the smooth, dark surface of the conference table and tapped her finger on it. "Told you it wouldn't be long before BODS found your match. Check him out."

Ariana didn't want to open the folder. The man inside on the profile wouldn't be Dillon. She just wasn't interested.

"Go on." Emma leaned across the table and flipped the file open. "He's good looking, is a certified public accountant and owns his own business. He likes yoga and going for long walks. And he likes cats. I sneaked a peek. He sounds perfect."

"Perfect" was Dillon, a man she felt like she'd known forever even though she'd just met him in the dark.

Emma pointed to the man's phone number. "Why don't you text him and see if he wants to go to the firefighter fundraiser tomorrow?"

"I don't know," Ariana hedged. "The fundraiser is an all-day event. I'd rather meet him for coffee. That way, if we don't connect, I can leave, and neither of us will be stuck with each other's company for hours."

"True, but it's for a good cause," Emma said. "And

the sooner you meet him, the sooner you'll know whether he's a fit."

"Fine," Ariana said. "I'll text him." She picked up her cellphone, praying Dillon would text her before she committed to a date with a complete stranger.

Dillon didn't call or text before she sent a text to —she looked at the profile—Jared Hill.

Would you like to meet tomorrow in Hellfire at the firefighter fundraiser?

She prayed he'd be busy and not respond until after Dillon called that night. *If* he called.

Her cellphone vibrated with a text message.

"Is it him?" Emma asked, leaning closer.

With a frown puckering her brow, she looked down at the message from Jared.

Yes. What time and where?

Her heart pounded in her chest. Now, she had a date with a man she didn't know while she was sure she was falling in love with one who wasn't her match.

Why had Dillon decided she should meet her match?

"Here, let me answer him." Emma keyed in a location and time and sent the text. "There you go. You're all set for tomorrow. How exciting!"

Ariana couldn't dredge up an excited bone in her entire body. "I guess I'd better get home and do the laundry, so I'll have something to wear." She rose from the table, looped her purse over her shoulder and gave all the ladies a hug before exiting the room. All the way down the elevator to the garage level, she regretted her decision to let BODS choose another match for her. She didn't want another match. If she couldn't be with Dillon, she'd rather be alone.

Now, she was stuck with a date for a day in Hellfire.

To end a perfectly awful day, Dillon didn't call her that night.

CHAPTER 12

DILLON PARKED his truck in a space in a field directed by volunteers in bright yellow vests. He'd worked late the night before and hadn't gone to bed until well after midnight. Too late to call Ariana, even if she'd wanted to talk to him. If he was honest with himself, he didn't feel much like talking anyway.

Mid-afternoon the day before, Emma had called to say Ariana had opted to meet her BODS match. Dillon had felt like he'd been sucker punched in the gut. When Emma had pushed again for him to meet his, he'd told her, "whatever." And "whatever" to Emma meant she could do what she wanted. And she wanted him to meet his BODS match.

"Just in case she's the woman of your dreams," Emma had said in a gratingly cheerful tone.

"Whatever," he'd repeated, not in the mood to talk to his sister, or anyone else for that matter.

The woman haunting his dreams was a petite little redhead who'd never ridden a horse or successfully landed a fish.

Later that afternoon, Emma had called him back. "Her name is Melanie Armstrong. She's five-feet-nine, brunette with brown eyes. Loves the outdoors, rides horses, runs marathons and is a personal trainer."

Great. She'd run circles around him and want him to run with her. He jogged, but not any farther than a couple of miles at a time. He didn't have the time to dedicate to run marathons.

"Oh, and I set it up that you two will meet at the Hellfire firefighter fundraiser. That way you don't have to worry about coming up with private conversations. You can just go enjoy the day and get to know each other in a casual environment."

"I'm thrilled," he responded.

Emma laughed. "You should be. She's ticks off every preference you listed."

"Damned list," he muttered.

"What was that you said?" Emma asked.

"Nothing. What time are we meeting?"

"In the parking lot at ten o'clock tomorrow morning," Emma said. "And Ariana will be there with her date. I hope you don't mind."

"Why should I mind?" Dillon barked. "She can go wherever the hell she likes."

"I thought maybe you two were getting thick,"

Emma said. "Though that doesn't make sense at all. You two weren't meant to match. You have nothing in common."

"Yeah. So you say."

"Do you doubt BODS?" Emma asked.

"I never completely bought into the idea that a computer program could pick a mate for me."

"You'll be pleasantly surprised tomorrow. I'm sure," Emma replied.

"Yeah. Gotta go. The plumbing just exploded somewhere."

"God, I hope not," Emma had said. "See you tomorrow."

So, here it was ten o'clock on Saturday, and he was going to meet a woman he had no desire to meet when he'd rather be with a woman who was meeting a man Dillon didn't know but wanted to slug in the face.

Yeah, his mood wasn't great, but it was all he had.

He climbed down from his truck, checked the BODS app on his phone for a photograph of Melanie Armstrong so that he could recognize her when he saw someone who looked like her.

Tall, dark and slender.

When he looked around the parking lot for a dark-haired woman, his gaze was drawn to a bright splash of red hair. Ariana? She stood by herself next to her vehicle, looking around the parking lot just like him.

He willed her to turn his way as he walked toward her. She didn't. Instead, she smiled and waved at a dark-haired, athletic man striding toward her.

Dillon's footsteps faltered, and he ground to a stop as Ariana held out her hand to the man and he smiled at her. He wore nice khaki trousers and a white polo shirt. He looked like a man who was comfortable in a boardroom or in a gym.

"Damn," he muttered.

"Dillon Jacobs?" a female voice said from behind him.

He turned to face a beautiful dark-haired woman with brown eyes. She wore form-fitting yoga pants, running shoes and a light blue tank top that fit her slender body to perfection Her hair was pulled back in a low ponytail, and her makeup was minimal and tasteful. She was just the kind of woman Dillon would have taken out on a date...before Ariana.

Now, all he could think about was how soon he could ditch her and head out to the ranch. He needed to muck stalls or ride out to the farthest pasture and pound some fence posts, anything to take his mind off another man putting his hands on Ariana's petite body.

He forced a smile for the woman. "Yes, I'm Dillon."

She held out her hand. "Melanie Armstrong."

When he took her hand in his, she squeezed hard, as if she had something to prove.

Dillon returned the pressure, a degree lighter. "Nice to meet you."

"Same. Thanks for picking a public location. You never know who you'll meet with dating services."

Dillon raised his eyebrows. "You do many of the dating apps?"

She shrugged. "I've tried a few. Leslie says hers is different. I hope so." She tilted her chin toward the tents, fire trucks and equipment displays. "This looks like fun. Leslie said there's games and competitions. I wouldn't mind joining. Where can we sign up?"

"They usually have the signup sheets at the fire station." He looked over her shoulder in the direction he'd seen Ariana. She was gone.

Just as well, he didn't need to ruin her date by staring at them all day.

"Come on, I'll show you where it is." He led the say to the station where they signed up for the tug of war, adding their names to a team halfway full. They also signed up for the three-legged race and the egg race.

"The tug of war is first," Mel said. "We should go find our team. We're on number five."

They found Team 5 and lined up alongside a rope stretched across a pit of mud.

"I didn't know they were going to get serious about this." Dillon looked skeptically at the pit. "We don't have to do this if you don't want to."

"I read the descriptions of the events and came

dressed to play." She smiled and lifted the rope. "Let's do this."

The other team fell in beside their end of the rope. When Dillon looked across at their competition, he had to swallow a groan.

Ariana and her date were in the middle of the team, holding the rope.

Her date gripped the rope like he knew what he was doing.

Dillon sized up both teams and smiled. His team had it in the bag. At the last minute, a woman joined his team. Okay. They had this, no problem.

The referee stepped up to the rope and settled a whistle between his lips. Before he could blow, another man approached the opposing team.

Dillon and his team groaned.

The man had to be six feet seven, if not taller, and probably weighed over three hundred pounds. He took a position at the end of their line and grabbed the rope in his big, meaty hands.

"It's about to get interesting," Mel said with a grin. "I hope you don't mind getting dirty."

The referee blew the whistle, and the teams leaned backward, digging their feet into the ground.

With the big guy on the other end, Dillon's team didn't stand a chance.

Inch by inch, Team 5 lost ground, although they fought valiantly.

The front member of the team soon approached the mud pit.

The big guy in the back of the other team, turned around, readjusted his grip and marched away from the pit, dragging along his team and Team 5. He didn't stop until all of Team 5 toppled into the pit, sinking into mud up to their knees.

Mel laughed, wiping mud from her face. She smiled at Dillon. "You're not muddy enough." She slung mud at him.

He ducked and the mud hit one of his other team members, and a mud fight ensued.

When he looked around for Ariana, she and her date had disappeared.

"That was fun," Mel said, mud in her hair and on her arms and light blue tank top. "What's next?"

"I believe the egg race is next." He wished they hadn't signed up for so many. He had to stay to finish the games when all he wanted to do was apologize to Mel, tell her it would never work out between them and then leave.

He walked with Mel to the next station where the egg race was to take place.

Mel leaned in as the referee explained the nature of the game.

One of a pair of competitors would place an egg between his or her chin and chest, run twenty yards to the other member of the pair and pass the egg without using their hands. The other person would run back to where the first person started.

Couples lined up on either side of the short field. Ariana joined the opposite line, picking a spot next to Mel. Her gaze met Dillon's as her date stepped into position beside Dillon.

Mel and Ariana were given raw eggs. They tucked them beneath their chins and waited.

The referee blew the whistle, and the ladies were off, running with their heads down toward Dillon and Ariana's date.

Others along the line dropped their eggs and fell out of the competition.

Ariana made it across the twenty yards to where her date stood a few seconds before Mel arrived in front of Dillon.

The swapping of the egg from one person to the other meant getting close. Really close, in order to get chins and chests in the game to make the transfer.

Dillon tried to focus on the egg beneath Mel's chin, but he was distracted by Ariana's date laughing as he tried to grab the egg with his chin.

"You got it?" Mel asked.

Dillon grabbed her shoulders and leaned sideways to get his chin beneath hers. "I think I have it," he said between gritted teeth.

Had Mel been Ariana, he would have stolen a kiss before he grabbed the egg. Hell, he might have said screw the egg and thrown the race just to get to kiss her longer.

He heard Ariana's squeal beside him and lost his concentration at the same time as Mel released her chin-hold on the egg.

The egg slipped.

Dillon grabbed for it with his chin and crushed it between his chin and chest getting raw egg goo all over his polo shirt.

Mel laughed. "Good effort," she said. "Now, we're a pair," she said, waving a hand toward his egg-covered shirt and hers, which was smeared with mud.

A soft gasp beside him made him glance toward Ariana. She had egg on her shirt and chin. Her date had yet to get anything on him. The volunteers handed out paper towels to the contestants. Ariana's date offered to wipe the egg off her shirt, but she took the towel from him and did it herself.

"Dillon, I'm so glad we caught up with you," Emma called out. She and Coop approached with Tag and Leslie trailing after them. After giving Dillon a head-to-toe glance, Emma grinned. "I take it you aren't fairing so well in the games."

"You could say that," Dillon said, forcing a smile.

Emma spotted Ariana, and stepped over to where she stood, working the egg out of her shirt. "Ariana, I don't think you've met Coop and Tag. Come and introduce us to your date." She hooked

Ariana's arm and brought her and her date over to the others.

"Y'all, this is Ariana Davis, a very good friend of mine," Emma announced.

Arianna's cheeks reddened as she turned toward the man in the khaki slacks. "This is my date, Jared Hill. Jared, this is Emma and Leslie…and Dillon."

EMMA TOOK up a position beside her man. "This is Frank Johnson, but we call him Coop." She waved toward Leslie. "The man with Leslie is Taggert Bronson, or Tag, to his friends." She turned to Dillon.

He tilted his head toward Mel. "My date, Melanie Armstrong."

Mel smiled. "Nice to meet you all."

"Are you signed up for the three-legged race?" Emma asked. "It's the only one I ever enter. I might even have a chance of winning this year with Coop as my partner." She stood on her toes, looking toward a group of people gathering. "I think it's time."

Dillon's gaze met Ariana's. She looked as miserable as he felt. Or was that wishful thinking on his part? He didn't want her to have fun with Jared. She should be with him. He still had to teach her how to fish and ride horses. And they had more pizza and apple pies to bake in his gourmet kitchen. And the hot tub hadn't been used since the last time they'd made love in it. This dating their perfect matches wasn't right. What made them so perfect, if they were miserable with them?

He turned to Mel to tell her he was done and wanted to leave. But he was too late. She grabbed his arm. "Come on, they're lining up. We have to get our gunny sack."

Dillon found himself being dragged toward the three-legged racecourse following Emma, Coop, Leslie and Tag.

A quick glance back assured him Ariana and Jared were coming, too.

When the race was over, he'd break it to Mel that he was leaving. If he could get Ariana alone, he'd tell her he was sorry he'd come with another woman and that he thought BODS had had it right the first time. He wanted her back.

A woman stood by the starting line, handing out burlap sacks to the couples participating in the race.

Mel took one and found a place for them on the starting line beside Coop and Emma. She dropped the sack on the ground and stuck her foot into it. "Come on, they're about to start."

Dillon put his foot into the bag beside Mel's and pulled the bag up to his knee.

"You have to put your arm around me," Mel said, dragging his arm around her waist. "We'll lead off with our outside feet."

He nodded, his attention on Ariana and Jared as

they got into position and Jared wrapped his arm around her waist.

Dillon's fists clenched. He wanted to storm over to Jared and demand he take his hands off his girl.

The problem was…Ariana wasn't his girl. He'd never spoken to her of commitment. He'd assumed it was too soon. In his heart, he knew it wasn't too soon for him. But Ariana had been through the death of her first husband. Did she need more time to consider a long-term relationship? With him?

The referee raised the whistle to his lips. "On your marks…get set…" and he blew the whistle long and loud.

The couples took off.

Dillon tried to lead off with the foot in the bag and almost tripped them both.

Mel helped him regain his balance, and then they took off after the others, regaining ground they'd lost in his clumsy start.

They passed several couples, caught up and passed Coop, Emma, Leslie and Tag.

Ahead of them Jared and Ariana were racing like a well-oiled machine, their legs moving in perfect unison.

Anger burned low in Dillon's belly. That should be him in the race with Ariana. He never should've let Emma talk him into bringing another woman to the fundraiser. He should've called Ariana and asked her to go with him before she'd agreed to go out with Jared.

With his arm around Mel, he pushed hard, determined to catch up to Jared and Ariana. Why it was so important, he didn't know. Just that he had to.

Ariana tripped and would have fallen, except Jared's arm tightened around her. He lifted her up and practically carried her across the finish line, coming in first.

Dillon and Mel were right behind them, finishing second. As they slowed, Dillon's foot got tangled in the burlap sack, and he pitched forward, taking Mel down with him. They landed on their knees.

Mel came up laughing, barely breathing hard.

Jared turned back to help, extending a hand to Mel. "Good job," Jared said. "You two run any races around here?"

"Yes," Mel said, releasing his hand. "I'm signed up for the Iron Man Marathon next month." She gave him a chin lift. "You?"

"I'm signed up for a marathon next weekend and the Iron Man next month as well." Jared's eyes narrowed. "Were you at the race in Galveston last month?"

She nodded. "I was."

"I thought you looked familiar." He held out his hand, again. "Nice to meet you, Melanie. We should compare schedules some time."

"We should," she said. Then she looked around to

where Dillon stood. "Is there something to drink around here?"

"There's a lemonade stand and a beer stand," Dillon said. "Choose your poison."

"I stay away from alcohol when I'm training for an Iron Man competition," Mel said. "Lemonade for me."

"Same," Jared said. His glance went to Dillon. "Let's get the ladies something to drink."

Dillon would rather tell Mel he was heading home, but he didn't want to do it in front of Ariana and Jared. "Fine."

The last thing he wanted was to make small talk with Ariana's date.

"So, are you a runner?" Jared asked Ariana.

She shook her head. "No. And I'd like a beer."

CHAPTER 13

ARIANA STOOD AWKWARDLY, watching the men disappear into the crowd. When she lost sight of Dillon, she couldn't help but study Melanie, Dillon's date.

The woman was everything a man could want in a life partner. She was tall, slender, athletic and gorgeous.

"He's cute, isn't he?" Melanie said, turning to face her.

"Yes, he is," Ariana said.

"I'll bet he runs every day of the week," Melanie said.

Ariana frowned. "I don't think so. He works long hours on construction sites. He has to be on his feet all day."

Melanie grinned. "I was talking about Jared. Although, Dillon's cute, too."

"Oh," Ariana said, feeling awkward and juvenile next to the tall woman.

"How long have you known Jared?"

"I met him today," Ariana answered.

"So, you aren't a runner?" Melanie asked.

"No. I prefer a low-impact exercise."

Melanie nodded. "I wonder what Jared does for a living."

"He's a corporate accountant," Ariana said, her gaze on the spot where she'd last seen Dillon before he disappeared.

"That's interesting." Melanie smiled. "I'm in corporate accounting, too. I'm the Chief Financial Officer of a small corporation."

Ariana stopped short of saying, *Are you fucking kidding me?*

Beautiful, tall, athletic and a CFO? She was perfect. Everything a man like Dillon could possibly want in a woman.

"Are you another one of Leslie's BODS clients?" Melanie asked.

Ariana swallowed a sob rising up her throat. "Leslie's my friend."

"But you say you just met Jared. Was that through BODS?" Melanie persisted.

"Yes. But it was a mistake. I'm not ready to date again." The sob lodged hard in her throat. "I can't do this."

"What's wrong?" Melanie asked, her brow creased with concern. "Did I say something to offend you?"

Dillon and Jared emerged from the crowd, each carrying lemonade and beer.

"Ariana, there you are," a voice said from behind her. She turned to find Dillon's brothers closing in on her.

When she turned back to Dillon, her pulse rate shot up and the lump in her throat made her feel like she couldn't breathe.

"Ariana?" Dillon approached, a frown pulling his eyebrows together. "Are you all right?"

"I don't know what I said," Melanie said. "We were talking, and then she got upset."

Dillon shoved the lemonade into Melanie's hand, tossed his beer in the trash and reached for Ariana.

She backed away. "I can't."

"Can't what?" Dillon asked. "Talk to me."

"I can't stand by and pretend to be okay when I'm dying inside." She waved a hand toward Melanie. "Look at her. She's perfect. BODS checked off every box on your preference list with her. She's beautiful."

"You're beautiful," he countered.

"She's a corporate executive."

"You own a business," Dillon said.

"She's outdoorsy."

"That doesn't have to mean everything." Dillon stepped toward her.

Ariana backed away.

"She's tall."

He gave her a gentle smile. "I've discovered a fascination with short women."

"I can't compete. BODS got it right this time." She turned to Jared. "I'm sorry. I can't pretend anymore. I'm not right for you. You deserve someone who will love you and all the miles you run. That person isn't me. I'm a yoga instructor, not a runner. I have to go," she said, the sobs rising up her throat. Ariana spun on her heels and bolted for the parking lot. She couldn't stay a moment longer when her heart was breaking into a million pieces.

"Stop her!" Dillon called out.

Colton, Brand and Ace stepped into her path, blocking her escape. When she tried to go around them, they moved, blocking her from leaving.

Dillon caught up to her, gripped her arms and turned her to face him.

Emma, Coop, Leslie and Tag joined them.

"What's wrong," Emma asked.

"I need to leave," Ariana said, her voice catching on a sob.

"Why?" Leslie asked.

"It didn't work. BODS didn't work," Ariana said, tears streaming down her face. She was embarrassed and past caring. "Jared isn't the one for me."

"Why do you say that?" Emma said. "Isn't he everything you listed that you wanted in a match?"

"He is, but that was then," Ariana whispered. "I

don't want that anymore." She looked up into Dillon's eyes. "I want what I can't have."

"And what is that?" Leslie asked her in a gentle voice.

"It doesn't matter." Ariana shook her head. "I'm not the right match for him."

"For me?" Dillon's hands squeezed her shoulders. "You're wrong, Ari. So wrong."

"But BODS found your perfect match. Melanie is everything."

Melanie shook her head. "Not if he doesn't want me."

"Ariana, BODS got it right the first time. We were matched for a reason," Dillon said. Then turning to Melanie, he said, "Mel, I'm sorry, but I've already found the one for me. It might have been a computer glitch, but Ariana is the perfect match for me. I don't care what BODS says now. It had it right the first time."

Ariana rested her hands on his chest. "But I'm not right for you."

"The hell you aren't." He pulled her into his arms and held her close against his body. "You fit me perfectly."

"I can never be taller," she said, sniffing.

"We're the same height where it counts," he said, pressing his lips against her ear and whispering, "in bed."

"We don't have anything in common," she said.

"You love homemade pizza and apple pie. So do I," he said.

"We don't have anything in common that counts," she countered.

"Pizza and apple pie count. The desire to have four or more children counts. Loving cooking together counts. Being willing to learn to fish counts." He cupped her face in his palms and brushed her cheeks with his thumbs. "Leslie's system did its job. It made me look at my life and prioritize what was most important."

Ariana looked up into his eyes, her own filled with tears. "And what is that?"

He brushed her lips with his. "Love."

Her heart constricted with the force of her feelings for him. "Isn't it too soon to fall in love?" she asked on a ragged breath.

"Not if you know it's right."

Hope blossomed in her chest. "And do you know?"

He nodded. "I know. I knew shortly after I bumped into you in the hallway. I'm pretty sure I love you, Ariana, and I would really hate it if you went off with Jared when he will never love you as much as I will."

"I'm not going off with Jared," Ariana said, her chest swelling with the love she felt for this man. "I'd rather be with you. I didn't want to give BODS another chance."

He crushed her in his arms and held her close.

"Okay, I have a confession to make," Emma said aloud, breaking into the tender moment between Ariana and Dillon.

Dillon loosened his hold on Ariana, if only a little. She stayed by his side, almost afraid he'd change his mind.

"What are you confessing, Emma?" Dillon asked. "Hurry and spill. I have some kissing to do."

"BODS was right all along," Emma said.

Ariana looked around Dillon to his sister. "What did you say?"

"BODS had it right the first time." Leslie stepped forward. "After we restored it and got the new server up and running, we ran the program, and it chose Dillon for you, Ariana, and vice versa." She smiled.

Ariana frowned. "Then why are we out with Melanie and Jared?"

"Yeah, why are we wasting our time with other people." He shot a look at Melanie. "No offense."

Melanie raised her hands. "None taken. I have a confession to make myself."

Dillon's brows descended. "More secrets?"

She gave him a crooked grin. "Emma put me up to pretending I was a BODS match."

Emma touched her brother's arm. "I wanted to be sure of your feelings for Ariana." She shook her head. "I'd guessed you were falling in love with her, but boy, I didn't realize just how far you'd fallen." She hugged him. "Ariana is perfect for you. And you're the right one for her. I couldn't be happier for you. I wanted you both to be sure for yourselves."

"If I wasn't so happy holding Ariana," Dillon said. "I'd strangle you, Sis."

"That was a pretty dirty trick to play on a friend, much less a family member." Ariana stared at Emma.

"I know. I was wrong. And don't blame Leslie. It was all my idea." Emma hugged Ariana. "Will you forgive me?"

Ariana wrapped her arms around Dillon's waist. "Maybe. Some day."

"In the meantime," Leslie turned to Melanie and Jared who stood beside each other talking in low voices. "BODS actually matched you two. Care to finish the date with each other?"

Jared grinned. "We've already negotiated terms and are working on the logistics." He nodded toward Ariana. "Thanks for bringing Mel and me together. We've discovered we've run many of the same races. We should know each other by now."

"We're headed to a juice bar back in Austin. Thanks for introducing us," Melanie said. To Dillon, she said, "It was fun, but I think you're in the right hands now. Don't let her go. She loves you."

Melanie and Jared left.

"If you don't need us to keep your woman in line, we have some beer to drink and friends to hang out with," Colton said.

"Yeah, and about BODS and female tricks," Ace sent a pointed look toward Emma, "you better not be messing with me when it's my turn at BODS. I won't play your games."

Emma held up a hand. "I swear, I won't monkey with a system that works."

Ace's eyes narrowed. "Not exactly the promise I was looking for."

"Don't worry. My meddling days are over," Emma said, drawing an X over her chest.

Ace smirked. "Yeah. I'll believe that when I see it." He waved as he, Colton and Brand wandered toward the beer tent. As they walked away, Ace and Brand pulled their wallets out, handing Colton a couple hundred dollars each.

"Are you two sticking around for the fireworks?" Emma asked Dillon and Ariana.

Dillon captured Ariana's gaze. "It's up to you. But I know of a place where we can set off some of our own fireworks."

"If it involves fireworks in a hot tub, I'm with you." With tears drying on her face and her heart bursting with hope and love for this man who'd bumped into her in the dark, Ariana couldn't be happier.

"Let's go home," Dillon said.

"Are we going to the ranch?"

He shook his head.

She looked up at him. "I thought you didn't consider the condo home."

"Anywhere I can be with you is home." He took her hand, waved at his sister and led Ariana away.

She couldn't wait to get home with Dillon. "Are we making pizza?"

"I think the only thing we'll be making tonight is love."

She laughed. "I think we have that recipe memorized."

EPILOGUE

"IT'S BEEN a month since Dillon took the plunge into BODS waters. Who's up next?" Emma asked.

The Jacobs brothers were lounging on the porch, drinking beer after a completely satisfying dinner of home-raised beef steaks, baked potatoes and corn on the cob.

"Can you give it a break, Emma?" Brand leaned his head back on the rocking chair and closed his eyes. "I, for one, am in no hurry to find a woman."

"Not every woman is like Stacy," Emma said. "She was clearly not a good match for you. BODS would never have picked her for you."

"You say that, but it would take a special woman to appreciate ranch life. Especially if she didn't grow up on one." Brand shook his head. "Nope. Once bitten, twice shy."

"You'll change your mind when BODS finds the right one for you," Emma said.

"I'd offer to go next, if Leslie would let me examine her code," Colton said. "I'm fascinated with what kind of algorithms she used."

"No way. BODS is Leslie's intellectual property," Emma said. "Just trust it. You need a woman in your life to balance your inner nerd."

"Why are you pushing this?" Ace asked. "You seem to be on a mission. Are you not telling us something?"

"As a matter of fact, there's a very good reason why I'm so determined to get my brothers married off." Emma turned to Coop and smiled.

"Are you going to tell us or keep us hanging in suspense?" Dillon asked from his seat on the porch swing, Ariana nestled up against him.

"You want to tell them?" Emma asked Coop.

He smiled and shook his head. "You tell."

"Someone tell us what's going on," Ace said. "I need another beer, and I'm not going in for it until you do."

Emma blurted, "Coop and I are expecting a baby."

Her brothers all pushed to their feet at the same time.

"You're expecting?" Ace asked.

Emma nodded, tears filling her eyes. "We are."

Ace pulled his sister into his arms. "Congratulations, Sis. We're happy for you."

One by one her brothers hugged her.

Dillon and Ariana were last.

"I guess you want some cousins to grow up with your little one," Dillon said. "That's why you're in such a hurry to marry us off...?"

She nodded, her hand going protectively to her flat belly. "I want my baby to know his uncles, aunts and cousins."

Ariana pulled Emma into her arms. "I'm so happy for you. For us. Our babies are going to grow up together."

Emma's eyebrows rose up her forehead. "Our babies?" She looked form Ariana to Dillon and back. "You're..."

"Expecting, too," Dillon confirmed, pulling Ariana into his arms. "Which means there's a wedding going to happen in the very near future. I expect all of you to be there."

"How?" Emma shook her head. "I know how. When?"

"We just found out. We figure in eight months," Ariana said. "Guess we'll be breaking ground on our house soon."

"A wedding, a new house and babies?" Dillon grinned broadly. "All because of a little software program called BODS." He shot a narrow-eyed glance at his remaining bachelor brothers. "So, what's keeping you? Are you afraid of the future?"

"Maybe," Ace said. "Aren't you? Have you ever changed a diaper?"

Dillon shook his head. "No, but I'm not afraid to try. It can't be any harder than cleaning a fish."

"Sweetheart, we're going to have to work on your analogies before the baby is born," Ariana said wryly.

"Which is back to the question," Emma said. "Who's brave enough to meet his match?"

When no one responded. Emma held up her hand. "Fine. We'll draw straws."

HELLFIRE, TEXAS

HELLFIRE BOOK #1

Elle James
New York Times Bestselling Author

All hell breaks loose when a firefighter
rescues a runaway

Hellfire, Texas

A Hellfire Story

NEW YORK TIMES BESTSELLING AUTHOR

ELLE JAMES

CHAPTER 1

THE HOT JULY sun beat down on the asphalt road. Shimmering heat waves rose like mirages as Becket Grayson drove the twenty miles home to Coyote Creek Ranch outside of Hellfire, Texas. Wearing only a sweat-damp T-shirt and the fire retardant pants and boots of a firefighter, he couldn't wait to get home, strip, and dive into the pool. Although he'd have to hose down before he clouded the water with the thick layer of soot covering his body from head to toe.

The Hellfire Volunteer Firefighter Association met the first Saturday of every month for training in firefighting, rescues, and first responder care. Today had been particularly grueling in the late summer swelter. Old Lady Mersen graciously donated her dilapidated barn for structural fire training and rescue.

All thirty volunteers had been on hand to participate. Though hot, the training couldn't have gone better. Each volunteer got a real taste of how fast an old barn would go up in flames, and just how much time they had to rescue any humans or animals inside. Some had the opportunity to exercise the use of SCBA, self-contained breathing apparatus, the masks and oxygen tanks that allowed them to enter smoke-filled buildings, limiting exposure and damage to their lungs. Other volunteers manned the fire engine and tanker truck, shuttling water from a nearby pond to the portable tank deployed on the ground. They unloaded a total of five tanks onto the barn fire before it was completely extinguished. With only one tanker truck, the shuttle operation slowed their ability to put out the fire, as the blaze rebuilt each time they ran out of water in the holding pool. They needed at least two tanker trucks in operation to keep the water flowing. As small as the Hellfire community was, the first engine and tanker truck would never have happened without generous donations from everyone in the district *and* a government grant. But, they had an engine that could carry a thousand, and a tanker capable of thirty-five hundred gallons. Forty-five hundred gallons was better than nothing.

Hot, tired, and satisfied with what he'd learned about combating fire without the advantages of a city fire hydrant and unlimited water supply, Becket had learned one thing that day. Firefighting involved a lot more than he'd ever imagined. As the Fire Chief said, all fires were different, just like people were different. Experience taught you the similarities, but you had to expect the unexpected.

Two miles from his turnoff, Becket could almost taste the ice-cold beer waiting in the fridge and feel the cool water of the ranch swimming pool on his skin.

A puff of dark smoke drifted up from a stalled vehicle on the shoulder of the road ahead. The puff grew into a billowing cloud, rising into the air.

Becket slowed as he neared the disabled vehicle.

A black-haired woman stood in the V of the open driver's door, attempting to push the vehicle off the road. She didn't need to worry about getting it off the road so much as getting herself away from the smoke and fire before the gas tank ignited and blew the car to pieces.

A hundred yards away from the potential disaster, Becket slammed on his brakes, shifted into park, and jumped out of his truck. "Get away from the car!" he yelled, running toward the idiot woman. "Get away before it explodes!"

The woman shot a brief glance back at him before continuing on her mission to get the car completely off the road and into the bone-dry grass.

Becket ran up behind her, grabbed her around the

middle, and hauled her away from the now-burning vehicle.

"Let go of me!" she screamed, tearing at his hands. "I have to get it off the road."

"Damn it, lady, it's not safe." Not knowing when the tank would ignite, he didn't have time to argue. Becket spun her around, threw her over his shoulder in a fireman's carry, and jogged away from the burning vehicle.

"I have to get it off the road," she said, her voice breaking with each jolt to her gut.

"Leave it where it is. I'll call in the fire department, they'll have the fire out before you know it. In the meantime, that vehicle is dangerous." He didn't stop or put her down until he was back behind his truck.

He set her on her feet, but she darted away from him, running back toward the vehicle, her long, jet-black hair flying out behind her.

Becket lunged, grabbed her arm, and jerked her back. "Are you crazy?"

"I can't leave it in the road," she sobbed. "Don't you see? He'll find it. He'll find me!" She tried prying his fingers free of her arm.

He wasn't letting go.

"The fire will ignite the gas tank. Unless you want to be fried like last year's turkey, you need to stand clear." He held her back to his chest, forcing her to view the fire and the inherent danger.

She sagged against him, her body shaking with the force of her sobs. "I have to hide it."

"Can I trust you to stay put?"

She nodded, her hair falling into her face.

"I'm making a call to the Hellfire Volunteer Firefighters Association."

Before he finished talking, she was shaking her head. "No. You can't. No one can know I'm here."

"Why?" He settled his hands on her shoulders and was about to turn her to face him when an explosion rocked the ground.

Becket grabbed the woman around the waist.

She yelped and whimpered as Becket ducked behind the tailgate of his pickup, and waited for the debris to settle. Then he slowly rose.

Smoke and fire shot into the air. Where the car had been now was a raging inferno. Black smoke curled into the sky.

"Sweetheart, I won't have to call 911. In the next fifteen minutes, this place will be surrounded by firefighters."

Her head twisted left and right as she attempted to pry his hands away from her waist. "You're hurting me."

He released her immediately. "The sheriff will want a statement from you."

"No. I can't." Again, she darted away from him. "I have to get as far away from here as possible."

Becket snagged her arm again and whipped her

around. "You can't just leave the scene of a fire. There will be an investigation." He stared down at her, finally getting a look at her. "Do I know you?"

"I don't…" The young woman glanced up, eyes narrowing. She reached up a hand and rubbed some of the soot off his face. Recognition dawned and her eyes grew round. "Becket? Becket Grayson?"

He nodded. "And I know I should know you, but I can't quite put my finger on it."

Her widened eyes filled with tears, and she flung her arms around his neck. "Oh, dear God. Becket!"

He held her, struggling to remember who she was.

Her body trembled, her arms like clamps around his neck.

"Hey." Surprised by her outburst, Becket patted her back. "It's going to be okay."

"No, it's not," she cried into his sweat-dampened shirt, further soaking it with her tears. "No, it's not."

His heart contracted, feeling some of the pain in her voice. "Yes, it is. But you have to start by telling me who you are." He hugged her again, then loosened the arms around his neck and pushed her to arms' length. "Well?"

The cheek she'd rested against his chest was black with soot, her hair wild and tangled. Familiar green eyes, red-rimmed and awash with tears, looked up at him. "You don't remember me." It was a statement, not a question.

"Sorry. You look awfully familiar, but I'm just not

making the connection." He smiled gently. "Enlighten me."

"I'm Kinsey Phillips. We used to be neighbors."

His confusion cleared, and he grinned. "Little Kinsey Phillips? The girl who used to hang out with Nash and follow us around the ranch, getting into trouble?"

Sniffling, she nodded.

Becket shook his head and ran his gaze over her from head to toe. "Look at you, all grown up." He chuckled. "Although, you didn't get much taller."

She straightened to her full height. "No. Sadly, I stopped growing taller when I was thirteen."

"Well, Little Kinsey..." He pulled her into the curve of his arm and faced the burning mess that had been her car. "What brings you back to Hellfire? Please tell me you didn't come to have your car worked on by my brother, Rider. I'm afraid there's no hope for it."

She bit her lip, and the tremors of a few moments before returned. "I didn't know where else to go. But I think I've made a huge mistake."

Her low, intense tone made Becket's fists clench, ready to take on whatever had her so scared. "Why do you say that?"

"He'll find me and make me pay."

"Who will find you?" Becket demanded, turning her to face him again.

She looked up at him, her bottom lip trembling. "My ex-boyfriend."

KINSEY'S SHUDDERED, her entire body quaking with the magnitude of what she'd done. She'd made a bid for freedom. If she didn't distance herself from the condemning evidence, all of her efforts to escape the hell she'd lived in for the past year, would be for nothing.

Sirens sounded in the distance, shaking her out of her stupor and spurring her to action. "You can't let them question me." She turned toward the still-burning vehicle. "It's bad enough this is the first place he'll look for me."

"Who is your boyfriend?"

"Ex-boyfriend," Kinsey corrected. "Dillon Massey."

"Name's familiar. Is he from around here?"

Kinsey shook her head, scanning the immediate area. "No, he's from Waco. He played football for Baylor a couple years ago, and he's playing for the Cowboys now."

"Massey, the quarterback?"

"Yes." She nodded, and then grabbed Becket's hands. "Please, you can't let anyone know I'm here. Dillon will make them think I'm crazy, and that I need him to look out for me." Kinsey pulled herself up straight. "I'm not. I've never been more lucid in my life. I had to get away."

Becket frowned. "Why?"

She raised her blouse, exposing the bruises on her ribs. "And there are more. Everywhere most people won't see."

His brows dipping lower, Becket's nostrils flared. "Bastard."

"You have no idea." Kinsey glanced toward the sound of the sirens. "Please. Let me hide. I can't face anyone."

"Who does the car belong to?"

Her jaw tightened. "Me. I'm surprised it got me this far. The thing has barely been driven in over a year."

"Why not?"

"He parked it in his shed and hid the keys. I found them early this morning, while he was passed out drunk."

"When they conduct the investigation, they'll trace the license plates."

She tilted her chin. "I removed them."

"Did you leave a purse with your identification inside the vehicle?"

"No. I didn't bring anything. I knew I'd have to start over with a new name."

"If there's anything left of the Vehicle Identification Number, they can track it through the system."

Glancing at the empty road, the sirens sounding

closer, Kinsey touched Becket's arm. "It will take time for them to find the details. By then, I could be halfway across the country. But right now, I can't talk to the sheriff or the firemen. If anyone knows I'm here, that knowledge could find its way into some police database and will allow Dillon to locate me. He has connections with the state police, the district courts, and who knows what other organizations." She shook her head. "I won't go back to him."

"Okay, okay." Becket rounded to the passenger side and opened the door. "Get in."

She scrambled in, hands shaking, her heart beating so fast she was sure it would explode like the car. Kinsey glanced out the back window of the truck. The road was still clear. A curve hid them from view for a little longer. "Hurry."

"On it." Dillon fired up the engine and pulled onto the blacktop, flooring the accelerator. They reached the next curve before the rescue vehicles appeared.

Kinsey collapsed against the seat back, her nerves shot and her stomach roiling. "That was close."

"Sweetheart, you don't know just how close. If emergency vehicles hadn't been coming, I would not have left. As dry as it's been, a fire like that could spread too easily, consuming thousands of acres if left unchecked."

"I'm sorry. I wouldn't have asked you to leave the scene, but I know Dillon. The last time I tried to leave, I was caught because he called the state police and had me hauled home."

"Couldn't you have gone to a hospital and asked for a social worker to verify your injuries?" Becket glanced her way, his brows furrowed in a deep V. "Women's shelters are located all over Dallas."

"I tried." She turned toward the window, her heart hurting, reliving the pain of the beating he'd given her when he'd brought her home. He'd convinced the hospital she'd fallen down the stairs. No one wanted to believe the quarterback of an NFL team would terrorize his girlfriend into submission, beating her whenever he felt like it. "Look, you don't need to be involved in this. If you could take me to the nearest truck stop, I'll hitch a ride."

"Where would you go?"

"Wherever the trucker is going."

He shook his head. "Hitchhiking is dangerous."

Kinsey snorted. "It'd be a cakewalk compared to what I've been through."

Becket sat silent, gripping the steering wheel so tightly his knuckles turned white. "Nash is part of the sheriff's department in Hellfire now. Let me call him."

"No!" She shook her head, violently. "You can't report me to the sheriff's department. I told you. Dillon has friends everywhere, even in the state police and Texas Rangers. He'd have them looking for me. If a report popped up anywhere in the state, they'd notify him immediately."

"When was the last time he saw you?"

"Last night. After he downed a fifth of whiskey, Dillon gave me the bruises you saw. I'm sure he slept it off by eight this morning. He'll be looking for me. By now, he's got the state police on the lookout for my car. He probably reported it as stolen. I wouldn't be surprised if he puts out a missing person report, claiming I've been kidnapped." Kinsey sighed. "Take me to the truck stop. I won't have you arrested for helping me."

"I'm not taking you to the truck stop."

Kinsey slid the window down a crack and listened. She couldn't hear the sirens anymore. Her pulse slowed and she allowed herself to relax against the back of the seat.

Becket slowed and turned at the gate to the Coyote Creek Ranch.

The entrance was just as she remembered. Rock columns supported the huge arched sign with the name of the ranch burned into the wood. She'd grown up on the much-smaller ranch next door. The only child of older parents, she'd ride her horse to visit the Graysons. She loved Nash and Rider like the brothers she'd never had. Chance had been a wild card, away more than he was there, and Becket…

As a young teen, Kinsey had the biggest crush on Becket, the oldest of the Graysons. She'd loved his longish blond hair and those startling blue eyes. Even now, covered in soot, his eyes were a bright spot of color on an otherwise-blackened face.

"I can't stay here," she said, looking over her shoulder. "Your wife and children don't need me dragging them through whatever Dillon has in store for me. I guarantee, repercussions will be bad."

"Don't worry about the Graysons. Mom and Dad are in Hawaii, celebrating their 40th anniversary. None of us brothers are married, and Lily's too stubborn to find a man to put up with her."

"What?" Kinsey glanced his way. "Not married? Are the women in this area blind? I practically worshipped you as a child."

Becket chuckled. "I remember you following me around when Nash and Rider were busy. Seems you were always there when I brought a girl out to the ranch."

Her cheeks heated. She'd done her darnedest to be in the way of Becket and his girlfriends. She didn't like it when he kissed and hugged on them. In her dreams, she'd been the one he'd fallen in love with and wanted to marry. But that hadn't happened. He'd dated the prom queen and married her soon after graduation.

"I thought you had married."

"Didn't last."

"Why not?"

"It's a long story."

"If I remember, it's a long driveway up to the ranch house."

Becket paused. For a moment, Kinsey thought he was done talking about his life and failed marriage. Then he spoke again. "After college, Briana wanted me to stay and work for one of the big architecture firms in Dallas. I was okay with the job for a while, but I missed the ranch."

"You always loved being outdoors. I can't imagine you stuck in an office."

He nodded. "Dad had a heart attack four years ago."

"I'm sorry to hear that, but I assume he survived, since they're in Hawaii."

Becket smiled. "He did, but he can't work as hard as he used to."

"So, you came home to run the ranch?"

"Yeah." Becket's gaze remained on the curving drive ahead. "Briana didn't want to leave the social scene. We tried the long-distance thing, but she didn't like it. Or rather, the marriage didn't work for her when she found a wealthy replacement for me."

"Wow. That's harsh."

"Eh. It all worked out for the best. We didn't have children, because she wanted to wait. I like it here. I have satellite internet. I telecommute in the evenings on projects for my old firm, so I stay fresh on what's going on in the industry. During the day, I'm a rancher."

"Sounds like you know what you want out of life." Kinsey sighed and rested her head against the window. "I just want to be free of Dillon."

"What about you? You went to Baylor. Did you graduate?"

"I did. With a nursing degree. I worked in pediatric nursing."

"Did you?"

"For a while. Dillon was still at Baylor when I graduated. When he signed on with the Cowboys, he changed. He said I didn't need to work and badgered me into quitting." Kinsey remembered how much she hated staying at home, and how useless she felt. "I loved my job. The kids were great."

Becket stared at the road ahead. "We leave high school with a lot of dreams and expectations."

"I figured I'd be happily married by now with one or two kids." Kinsey snorted.

"Same here." Becket's lips twisted. "We play the hands we're dealt. How long have you put up with the abuse?"

"Too long." Kinsey stared out the window. "The beatings started when he signed on with the NFL. He'd take me to parties. When his teammates paid too much attention to me, he'd get jealous, drink too much, and hit me when we got back to our place."

"Why didn't you leave him then?"

"In the morning, he'd apologize and promise not to do it again." Her lip pulled back in a sneer. "But, he did. Eventually, he stopped taking me to the parties." Her life would have been so different had she left him the first time he hit her. She'd been a fool to believe he would stop.

"Couldn't you have gone to your family?"

"Each time I mentioned leaving, Dillon flew into a rage and threatened to kill me. Then he took away my car. He said it was for my own good. The car was too old, and needed too much work to drive." At first, Kinsey had thought his action was out of concern for her safety. But her checkbook and credit cards disappeared, and he blamed her for being careless, forcing her to live off whatever pittance of cash he gave her. Without a job, she had no income and became a prisoner in Dillon's home. "He told me I was a terrible driver and shouldn't be on the road. That I'd probably end up crashing into someone."

"The man's a dick."

"Tell me about it." Kinsey bit her lip to keep it from trembling. "I think part of the reason he stopped me from driving was that I'd go to visit my parents. Like he was jealous of how much I loved them, and liked spending time at home. By taking away my car, he left me with no way of getting there. Mom and Dad came up to visit me in Dallas when they could, but after they left, Dillon would stomp around the house, sullen and angry. He'd accuse me of being a mama's girl. If I defended myself, he hit me."

"Your parents were good people," Becket said. "I was sorry to hear of the accident."

Tears slipped from Kinsey's eyes. "They were on their way to visit me, since I couldn't go to them. I think they knew I was in trouble."

"Why didn't you tell them what was going on?"

"I was embarrassed, ashamed, and scared. By then, Dillon was my world. I didn't think I had any other alternatives. And he swore he loved me."

"He had a lousy way of showing it," Becket said through tight lips.

She agreed. Along with the physical abuse, Dillon heaped enough mental and verbal abuse on Kinsey, she'd started to believe him.

You're not smart enough to be a nurse. You'll kill a kid with your carelessness, he'd say.

When her parents died, she'd stumbled around in a fog of grief. Dillon coerced her into signing a power of attorney, allowing him to settle their estate. Before she knew what he'd done, he'd sold her parents' property, lock, stock and barrel, without letting her go through any of their things. He'd put the money in his own account, telling her it was a joint account. She never saw any of the money— never had access to the bank.

Several times over the past few months, she had considered leaving him. But with her parents gone, no money to start over, and no one to turn to, she'd hesitated.

Then, a month ago, he'd beaten her so badly she'd been knocked unconscious. When she came to, she knew she had to get out before he killed her. She stole change out of Dillon's drawer, only a little at a time so he wouldn't notice. After a couple weeks, she had enough for a tank of gas.

Dillon settled into a pattern of drinking, beating her, and passing out. She used the hours he was unconscious to scour the house in search of her keys. She'd begun to despair, thinking he'd thrown them away. Until last night. He'd gone out drinking with his teammates. When he'd arrived home, he'd gone straight to the refrigerator for another beer. He'd forgotten he'd finished off the last bottle the night before and blamed her for drinking the beer. With no beer left in the house, he reached for the whiskey.

With a sickening sense of the inevitable, Kinsey braced herself, but she was never prepared when he started hitting. This time, when he passed out, she'd raided his pockets and the keychain he guarded carefully. On it was the key to her car.

Grabbing the handful of change she'd hoarded, she didn't bother packing clothes, afraid if she took too long, he'd wake before she got her car started and out of the shed.

Heart in her throat, she'd pried open the shed door and climbed into her dusty old vehicle. She'd stuck the key in the ignition, praying it would start. Dillon had charged the battery and started the car the week before, saying it was time to sell it. Hopefully, the battery had retained its charge.

On her second attempt, she pumped the gas pedal and held her breath. The engine groaned, and by some miracle it caught, coughed, and sputtered to life.

Before she could chicken out, before Dillon could stagger through the door and drag her out of the vehicle, she'd shoved the gear shift into reverse and backed out of the shed, scraping her car along the side of Dillon's pristine four-wheel drive pickup, and bounced over the curb onto the street.

She'd made it out, and she wasn't going back.

ABOUT THE AUTHOR

ELLE JAMES also writing as MYLA JACKSON is a *New York Times* and *USA Today* Bestselling author of books including cowboys, intrigues and paranormal adventures that keep her readers on the edges of their seats. When she's not at her computer, she's traveling, snow skiing, boating, or riding her ATV, dreaming up new stories. Learn more about Elle James at www.ellejames.com

Website | Facebook | Twitter | GoodReads | Newsletter | BookBub | Amazon

Or visit her alter ego Myla Jackson at
mylajackson.com
Website | Facebook | Twitter | Newsletter

Follow Me!
www.ellejames.com
ellejames@ellejames.com

Montana SEAL Daddy (#7)

Montana Ranger's Wedding Vow (#8)

Montana SEAL Undercover Daddy (#9)

Cape Cod SEAL Rescue (#10)

Montana SEAL Friendly Fire (#11)

Montana SEAL's Mail-Order Bride (#12)

SEAL Justice (#13)

Ranger Creed (#14)

Delta Force Rescue (#15)

Montana Rescue (Sleeper SEAL)

Hot SEAL Salty Dog (SEALs in Paradise)

Hot SEAL Hawaiian Nights (SEALs in Paradise)

Hot SEAL Bachelor Party (SEALs in Paradise)

Brotherhood Protectors Vol 1

Hellfire Series

Hellfire, Texas (#1)

Justice Burning (#2)

Smoldering Desire (#3)

Hellfire in High Heels (#4)

Playing With Fire (#5)

Up in Flames (#6)

Total Meltdown (#7)

Declan's Defenders

Marine Force Recon (#1)

Show of Force (#2)

Full Force (#3)

Driving Force (#4)

Tactical Force (#5)

Disruptive Force (#6)

Mission: Six

One Intrepid SEAL

Two Dauntless Hearts

Three Courageous Words

Four Relentless Days

Five Ways to Surrender

Six Minutes to Midnight

Hearts & Heroes Series

Wyatt's War (#1)

Mack's Witness (#2)

Ronin's Return (#3)

Sam's Surrender (#4)

Take No Prisoners Series

SEAL's Honor (#1)

SEAL'S Desire (#2)

SEAL's Embrace (#3)

Covert Cowboys Inc Series

Triggered (#1)

Taking Aim (#2)

Bodyguard Under Fire (#3)

Cowboy Resurrected (#4)

Navy SEAL Justice (#5)

Navy SEAL Newlywed (#6)

High Country Hideout (#7)

Clandestine Christmas (#8)

Thunder Horse Series

Hostage to Thunder Horse (#1)

Thunder Horse Heritage (#2)

Thunder Horse Redemption (#3)

Christmas at Thunder Horse Ranch (#4)

Demon Series

Hot Demon Nights (#1)

Demon's Embrace (#2)

Tempting the Demon (#3)

Lords of the Underworld

Witch's Initiation (#1)

Witch's Seduction (#2)

The Witch's Desire (#3)

Possessing the Witch (#4)

Stealth Operations Specialists (SOS)

Nick of Time

Alaskan Fantasy

Boys Behaving Badly Anthology

Rogues (#1)

Blue Collar (#2)

Pirates (#3)

Stranded (#4)

First Responder (#5)

Blown Away

Feel the Heat

The Heart of a Cowboy

Protecting His Heroine

Warrior's Conquest

Enslaved by the Viking Short Story

Conquests

Smokin' Hot Firemen

Love on the Rocks

Protecting the Colton Bride

Protecting the Colton Bride & Colton's Cowboy Code

Heir to Murder

Secret Service Rescue

High Octane Heroes

Haunted

Engaged with the Boss

Cowboy Brigade

Time Raiders: The Whisper

Bundle of Trouble

Killer Body

Operation XOXO

An Unexpected Clue

Baby Bling

Under Suspicion, With Child

Texas-Size Secrets

Cowboy Sanctuary

Lakota Baby

Dakota Meltdown

Beneath the Texas Moon

Made in the USA
Columbia, SC
09 February 2022

55795681R00128